PARADISE HILLS SUMMER

MERRI MAYWETHER

This book is a work of fiction. The characters, incidents, and dialogue are from the author's imagination and are not to be construed as real. Any resemblance to actual events or persons, living or dead, is entirely coincidental.

PARADISE HILLS SUMMER Copyright © 2019 Merri Maywether. Cover Design by Mariah Sinclair. All Rights reserved. Printed in the United States of America. This book or parts thereof may not be used or reproduced in any form, stored in any retrieval system, or transmitted in any form by any means—electronic, mechanical, photocopy, recording, or otherwise--without written permission of the publisher, except in the case of brief quotations embodied in critical articles and reviews, as provided by United States of America Copyright law.

All rights reserved.
978-169-78002-4-1

For permission requests address inquiries to:

Merri Maywether

P.O. Box 109

Sweet Grass, MT 59484

merrimaywether@gmail.com

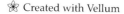 Created with Vellum

When people ask why I moved to Montana, my answer is always the same. I fell in love with a Montana Man...when he said he lived on a farm, I thought he was just trying to impress me. Randy, you are my better half.

Montana Kim, thank you for the adventures.
Missouri Kim, you make me a better storyteller.
Victoria, you live miles away, but it feels like you're my next-door neighbor.
I love you all,

Merri

1

THE PARADISE HILLS RESORT

Faith's job at the coffee kiosk at the Paradise Hills Resort entrance came to her in the least likely of circumstances. She had been a guest at the resort six months prior. If things had gone as planned, she would have been there on her honeymoon with the love of her life.

Instead, Faith stayed at the resort to hide from her friends and family after her fiancé called off the wedding. Breakups are hard. They are even worse in a small town. Everyone knew what happened, and it was hard to know whose side of the issue they chose until they said something. And then there was the mental preparation for sidestepping confrontation or derailing the pity that weighed more than a wet wool blanket. It was easier to go away and regroup and return home when she had her wits about her.

The day before Faith's scheduled return home, the barista named Misty slid Faith's small coffee across the counter. Before Faith picked up the cup, Misty inquired, "Would you be interested in working here?"

For years Faith helped her father manage the feed supply store. She was qualified. The question she never got to ask was, why did the woman who would go on to be her daily companion ask her?

"Our manager gave notice this morning. She had her baby boy a month early and has decided to stay home with him." Misty pointed toward a woman who disappeared into the door that led to the business office. "Right before you approached the counter, the hotel manager asked me to keep an eye out for someone to fill the position. What are the odds you would come to the counter right after she asked me?"

People visited the coffee kiosk at all times of the day. Faith wanted to say the odds were highly likely. But she held her tongue. It turned out to be the right thing to do in the situation.

Faith didn't know it at the time. Paradise Hills, Montana, had its own special magic. It wasn't the pull-a-bunny-out-of-the-hat magic. People believed in the power of love. It spoke to them. And, when it did, they listened. "It's a sign," Misty declared. "Unless you don't need a job. And then we are in the middle of an awkward conversation." Faith regarded the woman who wore bright red lipstick and held her hair pinned with a poinsettia headband with warmth. She was the opposite of Faith, who always wore her long brown hair in a sensible style of being parted to the side or pulled back in a ponytail. The more Faith compared the woman in front of her with the life that had brought her confusion, the more the idea of a move appealed to her. She could become her own person. Renewed by the unexpected gift presented to her, Faith set her coffee on the counter. "Where do I apply?"

2

TIME TO TELL THE TRUTH

It had been six glorious months since Faith left Castle Hill, Montana. She surveyed the scenery around her and marveled at the place that gave her a new life. The sun rested high above the mountains where Paradise Hills, Montana, was nestled. Tall trees and bushes dotted the area creating shelter from the sun without obscuring people's view of the mountain range that invited visitors for year-round activities. Paradise Hills wasn't too far from the town where Faith was born and raised. It was far enough to give her room to grow, yet close enough to visit her family for special occasions.

The glow from the afternoon sun warmed the back of Faith's neck. The slight burning sensation reminded her she was alive. For months, Faith functioned in a haze. The transition to independence had her already overactive mind working on overdrive. Thanks to the horse in front of her, Faith learned how to settle her mind.

At first, Faith visited the stable for the therapeutic effects of being around the horses. The scent of the hay and kicked-up soil reminded her of her life at Castle Hill before she got engaged. Horses didn't care if you had the perfect color of flowers or if your waist was a half-inch too wide. They read the rider's feelings and mirrored them. The first time Faith visited the stable, her now favorite horse, a chestnut mare named Skye, wouldn't have anything to do with her. Faith held out her hand to pet the horse's nuzzle. Skye backed away with a fierce determination to avoid the touch.

Faith, who still hadn't recovered from the rejection from her fiancé, took it personally. "C'mon back. I won't hurt you."

Skye shook her head and backed further away.

"Do you have something bothering you?" Faith looked up to see a petite woman dressed in denim pants and a leather jacket that fell somewhere around her thighs. The woman explained her question. "The horse can sense your distress. Horses can't speak, but they sure have a way of saying they don't want to deal with our emotional baggage." The woman came up alongside Faith. There was something about her freckled grin. Faith warmed to her instantly. "My name is Mischa." Mischa regarded the horse with a tilt of her head and returned her attention to Faith. "Is it a man or family?"

Not ready to disclose her baggage, Faith replied, "A little of both."

"Well, don't let them weigh you down," Mischa's eye color was darkened with wisdom that surpassed her years. She looked to be about thirty years old. Her eyes held knowledge beyond the typical issues of figuring out how to pay the bills and making sense of everyday problems. "I know it can be hard. If you let go of your problems for even a small bit of time, you'll find that you can handle them when you come back to them."

"What do I have to lose?" Faith grinned. She inhaled a breath. When she exhaled, she released the tension that tightened the upper portion of her gut. It unwound enough for her

Paradise Hills Summer

to sense the difference. Faith wondered how long the knot of pain had been there without her being aware of it. As though she sensed the difference, Skye trotted forward to approach Faith. That was the day Faith and Mischa became friends.

Faith drifted out of the memory and smiled. With or without Mischa, she visited the stables. Every time, Faith left with less baggage and a stronger sense of who she was as a person. The cinnamon-colored horse didn't care if Faith was perfect. She only cared if Faith was kind. Through the regular visits with Skye, Faith found her peace.

Willie, the yard manager, came up alongside Faith. He turned up his chin so she could see his light blue eyes shielded by the cowboy hat. "It's been a while since you've been out here." Willie was old enough to be her father. Years of working in the sun with animals had leathered his skin into a permanent tan. Faith guessed it made him look older than he really was.

"It hasn't been that long." Faith tried to remember the last time she'd been out to the stables. It was Easter. Now it was the middle of May. She grimaced in disappointment with herself.

The kind, older man didn't need to say anything. The tilt of his hat and redirection of his gaze toward the horse spoke for him. The mare dipped its head over the coral bars and nudged Faith. "Tell her."

"I'm sorry. Six weeks has been too long." Faith rubbed the mare's nose. "I got caught up with helping Holly plan her wedding." She remembered the stress involved with getting so many small pieces to work together. Holly and Mischa helped Faith pull her life together when she moved to Paradise Hills. It was fair that she reciprocated by offering her expertise.

Guilt pinched Faith. Helping with Holly's wedding had brought her forgotten issues to the surface, so Faith stopped by

5

the stables for horse therapy. What kind of friend was she? Faith answered her question. One who only stopped by when she needed to feel better. It wasn't true, but from the outside, that's what it looked like. "I'm sorry, Skye. I'll stop by this weekend for a ride."

"Is that a threat or a promise?" Willie's smile spread to his eyes.

"I'm bringing some apple fritters with me."

"A promise."

The tinge of residual sadness from her breakup with Clark faded. She was in a better place without him.

Her pocket vibrated. The mare bobbed its head in reaction. "Sorry about that, Skye." Faith retrieved her phone and showed the notification to Willie. "It's a text from Holly."

It read, "What are you wearing tonight?"

"I have a date tonight," Faith shared the reason for the call as though the horse would say, "Oh, that makes sense."

Skye snorted and walked away. Willie chuckled. "At least you know how she feels about the matter.

Mischa replied to the group text. "This will be so much fun. Looking forward to the friend time."

A knot formed in Faith's stomach. Something in her gut told her the date was a bigger deal than just meeting a guy that moved into town, which was why she visited the stables. To find her center. Skye trotted to the middle of the ring and refused to talk to Faith.

Willie cast a sideways glance at Faith and chuckled. "You said something wrong." Faith hoped the horse's reaction wasn't a sign of what was to come.

Paradise Hills Summer

FAITH CHECKED her reflection in the windows as she passed the different shops on Main Street. She didn't want to give her friends, or the mystery guy, any ideas that she was interested in a relationship, but she still wanted to look nice. The curled ends of her shoulder-length brown hair said nice but not too fancy. Her sheer pink blouse over a camisole with her jeans that had embroidered pockets gave her a boost of confidence. Faith had changed since moving to Paradise Hills. She didn't have to work so hard to feel good about herself.

Several of the stores had red, white, and blue flags and streamers decorating their storefronts. Paradise Hills always seemed festive. It was one of the many reasons Faith was satisfied with her move to the picturesque town. People worked together to make something special.

Before Faith knew it, she was in front of the cafe. Faith checked her step tracker. Even with the dawdling over her hair and makeup, she arrived at the cafe ten minutes early. She rehearsed the events in her mind. They were having dinner at the cafe. That would take an hour. After that, the group of friends would go to the new virtual shooting range on the other side of the movie theater. They displayed different life-size scenarios on a big screen. Participants in the game played the role of a spy, police officer, or old-time sheriff. If she were having fun, that would be another hour. If she weren't, she'd beg off at half-hour. Taking the walk home into consideration, Faith would be home by 9:30 or 10:00 at the latest.

Faith opened the door, and the scent of freshly baked apple pie wafted through the air. Her eyes crossed over the rows of wooden tables decorated with red, white, and blue carnation centerpieces to the family table in the back corner. Faith froze and blinked to push away what she thought she saw. What were the odds that her ex-fiancé, looking better than she

7

remembered, would be at the table she assumed was reserved for her friends?

The first thing that came to Faith's mind was this had to be a mistake. Another brief thought flickered like a lightbulb in its last stages of lumination. A nightmare. She was having a nightmare.

Months ago, Faith watched a documentary on dream therapy. The narrator said the trick to controlling a dream was to remind yourself that the situation was a figment of your imagination. She closed her eyes. With all her heart, she told herself, "This is a dream," she whispered. "It is nerves. Holly and Liam's wedding is bringing my hidden issues to the surface." Faith's heart jumped into her throat, and she did what any sane person would do. She turned to run.

Except, she didn't get too far. Through the window, she saw her companions for the unavoidable disaster. Mischa and her boyfriend Kellen were on the other side of the half-wooden door. They smiled their greeting as they came through the entrance to the café. Mischa walked into Faith and wrapped her arms around Faith's shoulders. With the gentle squeeze, warmth radiated through Faith. Faith exhaled. Her heart knew it would be okay, and when she turned around, Clark would not be there.

"How was your day?"

Mischa's warm personality couldn't be contained. Faith resisted the urge to turn and check if the ghost of relationships past was still in the corner of the room. "Ah. Interesting. My day was interesting. How was yours?"

Kellen touched Mischa's shoulder. "Clark's here."

With the confirmation of her worse fear coming true, Faith clamped her mouth shut and swallowed. Kellen continued his course and was halfway to the table when Clark rose to greet

Paradise Hills Summer

him. Mischa tilted her head to nudge Faith to join them at the table.

Faith pasted a smile on her face. "I have to go to the bathroom."

The bathrooms in the cafe were toward the back of the restaurant. Saloon style, wooden doors separated the entryway to the two rooms. Faith focused on her destination and rushed by the group that had converged at the table. On the way there, she noticed that Clark had changed. When she left him, he was a regular guy with regular stature. Now he looked like one of those men working to qualify for one of those world's strongest men's competitions. His biceps stretched the sleeve of his black t-shirt.

"Why, why, why?" Faith moaned to herself. Not only had life thought it was time to address her issues, but it also came in the form of her ex looking better than ever. Given the population density, Faith knew the eventuality of running into Clark. They came from a small town that was less than an hour from Paradise Hills. In the recesses of Faith's mind, she hoped that when it happened, Clark would look worse for the wear, that her absence had struck him so deeply he found it hard to go on with his life. The man she got a passing glance at was a remodeled version of the man who left her. His presence proved the last thing he said to her. "I would be better off without you." The humbling from him being right was more than she thought she could bear.

Faith braced herself with her hands against the edge of the bathroom sink and took in her surroundings. The slate gray walls had a grapevine wreath with flowers braided in the branches. Beneath the wreath, someone had etched a quote in a curvy font on the wall. "When all else fails, get a second piece of pie." Faith snickered at the lack of relevance to her particular situation. She was hiding in the bathroom to find the

9

wherewithal to deal with an uncomfortable situation. Two pieces of pie was all life gave her?

"It's time to tell the truth." Faith sighed, inhaled deeply, and reached for the door to deal with the situation. Holly and Mischa's concerned faces were on the other side to greet her. Faith grimaced to show her discomfort. "I don't know how to tell you two this. I think I caught a stomach bug."

3

SOMETHING YOU'D LIKE TO SHARE

"Before you go home with this, ahem, mysterious illness." Holly's voice softened to relay her concern. "Is there something you want to share?"

Faith pursed her lips. It wasn't like she lied. When asked, she told people she moved to Paradise Hills after a breakup. She just withheld the minor detail that it was with her fiancé.

She called Clark after reading through a chain of confusing text messages he sent. With no explanation whatsoever, he broke up with her. Because he was driving when he was angry, he rolled his pickup truck. It went from bad to worse from there.

Faith's hands became interesting. She cast a glance toward her friends and brought her gaze back to fingers that had been without a ring for months. "I may have forgotten to mention that I was engaged."

"You forgot to mention that you were engaged to that sculpted specimen of a human being?" Mischa wasn't as sympathetic as Holly.

"He didn't look like that when we were together," Faith half whined, half grumbled.

true. The Clark she left behind had always been a
ı. His go-to outfit was an oversized t-shirt, some
dirty jeans, and either a cowboy hat or a baseball cap. The only
time he didn't wear a hat was when he was at church or the
dinner table. The man at the table looked like he belonged in a
men's fitness magazine.

"It makes sense," Holly's voice was breathy with revelation. "All the Pinterest boards with wedding ideas."

"Yes," Mischa added. "I wondered why someone who didn't date had the most organized Pinterest page I have ever seen."

Faith had over twenty wedding categories on her Pinterest page. It had ideas for dresses, decorations, and music playlists but got as specific as nail polish colors. If Faith had made it to the altar, her wedding would have been perfect.

The shifting light behind them caught both Holly and Mischa's attention. "We'll talk about this later." Holly emphasized the last word while stepping away from the door. As best as Faith could tell from her friend's reaction, the situation caught her friends unaware of all the details of the guest list too.

Clark's face peeked into the empty doorway. His whiskey brown eyes homed in on Faith, and a crooked grin spread across his face. It was the same grin that got Clark out of trouble more times than Faith could remember. His full body appeared in the doorway. "Imagine meeting like this." Clark pulled on his ear. It was a habit he developed when they were in fourth grade. Faith never told him, but that's how she could tell when Clark was trying hard. It was like he was opening his ears to wisdom delivered on a frequency that could only be accessed if he changed the position of his ear.

"Yes," Faith squeaked. Her mind had come to a standstill. She didn't know what to say or do. She cleared her voice,

Paradise Hills Summer

"Long time no see." With Clark standing in front of her, Faith took advantage of the situation to take in his full image. Clark had to have gained twenty pounds of muscle and a ton of confidence. Her small-town sweetheart had grown into a hunk of a man.

The corners of Clark's mouth curved to form a slight smile, and he tilted his chin toward her. "You look good."

"I can say the same for you." Faith's heart ached. She foolishly believed that erasing all images of Clark would help her forget how to love him. Now that Clark was standing before her, Faith found herself wrong again. She wanted everything to be right between them. For Clark to approach Faith and take her by the hand and say something like, "Let's work this out." Except it was too late. Clark and Faith were beyond working things out. Faith made sure of it when she left Castle Hill without a backward glance.

The echoes of the last time Clark and Faith talked kept her glued to the spot where she stood. The tone in the echo cut deeper than the comfort Clark's warm grin offered. The tender scar her heart had formed throbbed with the remnants of the ache of their breakup. Faith's stomach twisted, and the awareness of her lie of having a stomach problem coming to fruition rose. It took a conscious effort to hold down the lunch she had eaten hours ago.

The voice that used to warm Faith chilled her. "Are you going to come out of here anytime soon?"

What was up with the smile? Was he making fun of her? Then it clicked. Faith's reaction amused him. Clark's presence sent her skittering like a mouse that had been caught stealing away a piece of cheese. By doing so, Faith had all but admitted Clark held the power cards. "Yes," she stammered. "Before you came in," she gestured in the direction where Holly and Mischa headed to emphasize her point, "I was telling Holly and Mischa that it might be better if I went home. Something I ate today didn't agree with me." The room grew warmer by the minute.

Clark had the good sense to frown in concern. "Oh, I'm sorry to hear you don't feel well. I was hoping to catch up with you."

Clark's reaction upturned Faith's world. She left Castle Hill, Montana, because he called off their engagement a week before the wedding day. Now, he wanted to catch up with her? It was more likely, he wanted to prove that he was better off without her. Faith pressed her hand against her stomach. She forced a grin and connected her eyes with his.

Memories Faith suppressed surged to the forefront of her mind. They were in the fourth-grade riding bicycles on the country dirt roads. Clark stood while he pedaled to keep ahead of her. Faith worked just as hard to keep up with him. He glanced back. His face tightened in determination, and he widened the gap between them. Those days ended with the bicycles being set against a tree and both of them swimming in a pond. One time when Clark and Faith were sitting on a fallen log, Clark leaned in to remove something from Faith's hair. The next thing Faith knew, he kissed her. It was a sweet peck on the lips. When Clark pulled away, he grinned shyly.

That was the day Faith Alexander knew she would marry Clark Grayson. Twenty years later, he stood there in front of her with the same sweet, shy expression. Except, Faith didn't want to love Clark anymore. Older and wiser, she didn't accept the simplicity of love. People didn't fall in love and go on to their happily ever after. Loving Clark Grayson had been messy and complicated and required a level of strength Faith lacked. For the entirety of their relationship, Clark created a gap for her to forge. Every time, Faith did it. She met Clark where he was, and when she caught up to him, he rewarded

Paradise Hills Summer

her with affection and gestures of admiration. Until one day, he didn't. Clark's disapproval hurt more than Faith cared to admit or remember. Faith cleared her throat, that had swollen. "Maybe another time."

"I could ditch this get-together and take you home," Clark offered.

"I'll be fine." The bathroom was getting too small. "I should go." Faith sighed and hurried to get around Clark. He moved to make room for her. She caught a whiff of his cologne when she passed him and immediately recognized his scent. The woody fragrance with hints of musk mixed in made her head float. It was the same one Clark wore when he proposed to her. The thought of him wearing it to meet another woman repulsed Faith. The stomach problems Faith fabricated turned to reality. She approached the small group of friends who had converged at the table. "I'm sorry to bail. I'll catch up with you later."

"Are you sure you can make it home?" Holly asked, "Your face looks like you've seen a ghost."

Technically, Faith had.

"I can take her home," Clark offered. "When she gets like this, she needs a cup of chamomile tea and crackers."

Faith whipped around to address Clark. He was right. Chamomile and crackers always settled her stomach. However, she'd rather get into a car with stranger danger than spend time with Clark Grayson. Faith swallowed the bitterness that rose in the back of her throat in a gulp and waved Clark away. "I don't want to infringe on your fun. Stay with them and go on with what you planned."

His eyes bore into hers. "I want to take care of you." The intensity behind the golden-brown irises and the sincerity in Clark's voice pushed for Faith's permission to let him back into her world. The roles had changed. Faith was ahead of

Clark. He was the one behind the gap, and it was her turn to lead him to the metaphorical pond. Except Faith wasn't having it. With her luck, once she let Clark in, she'd drown.

"I'm just going to get under a blanket on the couch and sleep." Clark closed Faith out of his world. Now it was time for her to show that she accepted his decision with dignity.

Somewhere between the bathroom and the table, his tone changed. He picked up where Clark and Faith left off as though the months they'd been apart hadn't happened. As far as Clark was concerned, they were having a tiff. "I'll make sure you'll get there. Then both of us will be happy." The familiar tone he used annoyed Faith.

Faith was about to say he was the last person she wanted to help her when a promise she made to herself stole her voice. For as long as Faith lived, she would never make a person feel as unwanted as Clark Grayson had made her feel. When Faith made that promise, she never imagined her first time to practice what she preached would be on the person who taught her the lesson.

4

KIDNAPPER, SERIAL KILLER

"We hear about times like this," Mischa gasped, "and we never think it will happen to us."

Good point, Faith thought to herself. She read a book about a couple who had a horrible fight. Faith hated the husband for how poorly he treated his wife. Come to think of it, Clark was in the same category of a jerk as the guy in the book. The husband followed his wife into the ladies' room to make amends. Faith judged the woman. Yet there she was, living it. When she got home, she would write a note to the author.

"People get stomach bugs all the time," Kellen dismissed Mischa's concern. "Or, Faith could have drunk too much coffee."

"No!" Mischa hit her boyfriend in the arm. Faith was so absorbed in avoiding Clark she hadn't noticed until now that Kellen and Mischa were wearing matching shirts. He wore a button-down long, sleeve black shirt. She wore a feminine version of the same thing. Mischa leaned toward Holly and wagged her eyebrows. "We never came up with a safety signal."

Holly frowned to show her confusion.

"A signal so we'd know if a person was in danger," Mischa pressed.

"Couldn't they just say it." Kellen rolled his eyes.

"Not when the serial killer, kidnapper, is right beside her." Mischa tried enlisting the help of Holly's fiancé, Liam. "Please tell them how the things they write in movies came from someone's real-world experience."

"She's a conspiracy theorist," Kellen apologized to Clark and Liam.

"That doesn't mean I'm wrong," Mischa's voice went up a notch. "Look at him. He's a hulk. Faith was trying to leave when we arrived."

All eyes landed on Clark, whose cheeks grew a deeper shade of red with each comment.

"I could call him a lot of special words," Faith took up Clark's defense, "serial killer, kidnapper is not one." When her comment failed to elicit the response she expected, she added, "He's more of a heartbreaker, wedding dodger."

"I'm not buying it," Mischa replied. "What if he came here to get you back?" She pointed at Clark. "What are your intentions toward Faith?"

Clark directed his attention toward Faith. Disappointment in the obvious answer changed his voice by a full pitch. "You didn't tell them about me?"

"Do you know where he lives?" Mischa demanded.

Liam held his hand by his shoulders. "I'm not contributing to your paranoia."

They were at a crossroads.

Faith didn't want to eat at the restaurant.

Clark insisted he knew how to nurse her to health.

Mischa suspected "nurse her to health" included kidnapping or murder.

Liam thought his relationship with Clark was enough of a reference to garner their trust.

In short, Clark and Faith's not-so-blind date ended with the agreement that they'd all get their food to go.

Thirty minutes later, Faith looked around her living room with five people sitting around her coffee table eating out of takeout boxes. Faith couldn't count on her hand the times she wondered if her house was big enough for company. In the six months she lived there, she'd had Mischa and Holly over. Otherwise, she kept to herself. It turned out her living room comfortably sat five people. Clark, Liam, and Holly sat on the plush maroon sofa. Kellen and Mischa sat in matching chairs on the other side of the old fashion trunk she used as a coffee table. Faith, who sat Japanese style on the carpet, surveyed the walls around them. They were dotted with collages of pictures of friends and family. Clark conspicuously was not in any of them. Faith looked at the clock she had positioned by the front door to make sure she left for work on time. She tipped her chin at the clock to acknowledge the irony. She had made it home before 9:00.

Occasionally, Mischa threw a suspicious glare in Clark's direction. It awed Faith every time it happened. Three months ago, when Kellen met Mischa, she was a timid person who did little to rouse any attention. Yet, here she was, a chihuahua snarling at a St. Bernard. Either Clark was oblivious, or he ignored Mischa's idle threats.

"If you don't mind my asking," Mischa picked off a piece of cake and placed it in her mouth. She bobbed her head and gestured with her finger. "I should have waited to ask before I put that in my mouth." After she swallowed her bite, she continued, "How did you two meet?"

Clark's eyes met with Faith's. They both asked the same question. Do you want to tell them, or should I? The twinkle in

Faith's eye gave Clark the go-ahead to speak. He said, "The first day of kindergarten."

"We suspected." Kellen faced Mischa, and they nodded their agreement.

Faith could imagine the conversation they had in the car on the way to her house. She rode with Liam and Holly, who had a heated discussion about whether Liam was aware of the relationship between Clark and Faith. It turned out he knew.

Mischa's lip formed a thin line of disapproval. "When did you connect? As in, when did you two mutually decide you liked each other?"

"Oh, let me see," Clark rubbed his close-shaven beard. "I'd say it was the Christmas dance of our freshman year. I wanted to ask Faith to go, but Chris Brubaker asked first."

Until Clark had mentioned it, Faith had forgotten about the Christmas dance. For a writing unit, their teacher made the class write holiday poems. Under the guise of asking Faith to make sure his poem flowed well, Chris asked Faith to the dance. It was the topic of discussion for days. Chris had set a standard that frustrated the other boys in the class. Faith glowed with pride. She was as equally horrified when Chris ended up in the hospital with a ruptured appendix. With permission from Chris, Clark took Faith to the dance.

Clark used gel to part his hair to the side and wore too much Axe body spray. She recalled the polite conversation Clark had with her father. Flattered by the effort he put into the date, Faith fell irrevocably in love with Clark. She couldn't believe a guy like him would do so much for someone like her. Not when there were so many other girls who were prettier and more athletic than Faith.

"From then on, I learned to keep close to Faith." Clark's face darkened. "Until I forgot."

Prickles of awareness slid across Faith's shoulders. It was

Paradise Hills Summer

her turn to comment on Clark's story. Once, she had been foolish and believed she had earned his love. That would not happen again. Not one to dwell in the past, Faith focused on the present. "Does anyone want a cup of decaf? Tea?"

"Shh, he was getting to the good part," Holly swiped at Faith's attempt at creating a diversion.

"It may be the good part for you," Faith grumbled. "I've spent the past six months wishing I could forget." The best she had done was to reach a semblance of peace with the way things were. Sadly, as soon as she found herself in a good place in her life, Clark reappeared and disrupted the settling.

All eyes shifted to Clark. "I've spent the past six months with constant reminders of how I ruined a good thing." He turned to Faith. "One day, I was in the store to get some apple cider vinegar for my mother's potato salad."

"Who puts apple cider vinegar in their potato salad?" Mischa's face contorted like she had tasted something unpleasant.

"My mom does," Holly replied. "The real question is, who doesn't?"

"If it doesn't have mayonnaise, can it be called a salad?" Liam had chosen sides in the discussion.

Thinking about Betsy Grayson's German potato salad with double the bacon made Faith's mouth water. Every time Clark's mother entered a contest, she won. She had a wall of blue ribbons from local cook-offs to prove it.

Clark's rejection hurt. His mother's silence confirmed Faith's decision to leave Castle Hill. Betsy Grayson's denunciation was the equivalent of social banishment. Clark's voice pulled at Faith's attention. She tuned in to hear him say that Chris Brubaker was the manager of the local general store. Faith blinked and was back in her apartment with her friends.

"While he rang up my bill, Chris asked me what I did to

chase you out of town. I told him to mind his own business and charge me for the vinegar." Clark's jaw tightened. "Then, the wiseacre asked if I'd repay the favor from high school and give him your number."

Faith could relate to Clark's frustration. She had to change her number because people called to ask for her blessing to date Clark. Small towns could be brutal when it came to a breakup.

Clark pointed toward the picture of Faith with her friends. "I have one group of people labeling me a bailer." He gestured with his hand to point out Mischa. "And the other, calling me a kidnapping, serial killer."

"The more he talks, the more he fits the part."

"Mischa!" Holly, Liam, and Kellen exclaimed.

"On that note," Faith rose to clear away the empty food containers. She had played with her food because she didn't have the stomach to eat anything, so her soup container was still full.

"I'll help you," Clark took three of the to-go containers before Faith had the time to argue. He was still faster than her. Faith frowned. She didn't want Clark's help, but what else could she do? Start an argument in front of her friends? She begrudgingly led Clark to her kitchen on the other side of the living room wall. When they were out of sight of their friends, Clark whispered, "I still need to talk to you."

Faith whispered back, "I don't want to talk to you."

Clark reached into his pocket and retrieved his wallet. He took out a tattered envelope and handed it to Faith. "We need to talk about this so we both can have closure."

Faith eyed the letter. What if it was some legal document? And, once she accepted it, was bound to a courtroom resolution. It seemed crazy, but people sued each other all the time. Why should she be the exception to the rule?

Paradise Hills Summer

"This will clear up where things went wrong." Clark held it out further for Faith to accept.

Faith examined the envelope for hints of what it contained. She fumbled the envelope between her fingers. "What is this?"

"The reason I broke up with you. But you never got it."

5

SHH, THEY'RE MAKING UP

"We should get back out there," was on the tip of Faith's tongue. She didn't want to be alone in the kitchen with Clark for any more time than she had to be. They were already in there longer than it would have taken to drop some containers in the trash.

She heard Mischa's whisper, "Shh, they're about to make up."

"I thought you didn't like him." Kellen's job as a firefighter had all but erased his quiet voice.

Silence followed the simultaneous hiss of, "Be quiet."

"I set it in the bouquet I gave you. My mother said they found it in the space between the seat and the emergency brake." Clark shrugged. "Obviously, you never got it." He nudged his head to encourage Faith to open the letter. The concern in Clark's eyes made Faith's heartache. What information could have been on the other side of a tattered envelope?

Faith remembered the flowers. Clark dropped them off the day before the blowup. His eyes gleamed with what Faith interpreted to be love. The heat in his kiss had Faith thinking she was the luckiest girl in the town. It made Clark's behavior the next day that much harder to understand. It came out of nowhere. Faith forced a butter knife through the small opening and slit through the seal. Clark had used college-ruled paper to write his note.

Faith,

When I was thirteen, I knew you would be my wife. I didn't know how or when it would happen. I just knew you would be by my side forever. Our family and friends have been there every step of the way, helping us make the decisions that got us to where we are today. For that, I'm thankful. But marriage is between two people. You and me.

I know the flowers, the dress, the food is all for them. As long as you're my wife, I don't care if we have fish, steak, or hot dogs.

Before we get started with them, I want to have an us. A moment when we can say that was the beginning of Clark and Faith Grayson. Meet me at the courthouse on Wednesday at 4:00 for a private ceremony. It'll be just you and me. Then we can have the family and friends show.

I love everything about you.

Clark.

Faith's heart sank. Her mind raced so quickly she had to reread the letter a second and a third time. Each time it erased and replaced the answers she used to fill in the blanks for: Clark's outburst declaring Faith was only with him for show; His insistence that if Faith loved him, she would have been there when it mattered; His pained admission that they weren't suited for each other.

His mother, in a show of support for her son, banned Faith from Clark's hospital room. Her tight-lipped, "I'd prefer you didn't talk to him at all," stunned Faith into submission to Clark's will.

Each gesture became a nail for the coffin where Faith buried their relationship. From there, she mourned the loss of the love of her life.

Faith shifted her gaze from the note to Clark and back to the note. Because of Clark's silence, the course of their lives changed in a way neither had imagined. Her eyes traveled up the lines of script for one last read-through to the gap between them and landed on Clark's face. "Why didn't you say something to me?"

"I was afraid to see your face if you said no or tried to talk me out of it." He sighed. "Instead, I learned the hard way. No isn't half as bad compared to what I said."

He was right. Faith silently agreed. His "I'm not in love with the person you've become" was the equivalent of pulling her heart out of her chest and crushing it in front of her.

Clark's continuation broke Faith's reverie. "Then, you disappeared. Your family refused to speak to me or my parents. Talk about getting what you asked for."

Kellen's voice boomed, "He's talking about Karma."

"We know," Mischa whispered. "For the record, I told you something was off. How did he find her?"

"Are you serious?" Liam exclaimed. "We set them up on a date."

Paradise Hills Summer

"I'm talking about him knowing to come to Paradise Hills." Mischa hissed.

"I helped him get the job at the resort."

Faith could imagine Liam raising his hand while making a face at Mischa. The tension in the living room released the pressure to respond to Clark. "You know we can hear you in here," Faith called into the other room.

"Shh, she can hear us," Mischa echoed Faith.

Faith heard Liam's eye roll in his voice. "I know. I heard her."

From the outside looking in, the small group of people that made up Faith's world was perfect. Liam, a Hollywood star, found the love of his life last Christmas in a way that most people only read about. As a teenager, Kellen saved Mischa from a car accident. They reunited years later and instantly became a couple. Once anyone spent a considerable amount of time with Faith's friends, their definition of perfect would change. They all had their quirks, like believing in magic trees or creating conspiracies. On the whole, they were good people who tried to help each other through the intricacies of life.

Faith apologized with her eyes to Clark and moved to walk around him to join her friends in the other room. It didn't matter that she was still in love with Clark. He misjudged her, broke her heart, and left it to her friends to pick up the pieces. Clark said he came so they could have closure. As much as Faith wanted to argue, she knew he was right. Both of them had gaping wounds from the breakup. Faith had to admire him. This was at the top of the list of uncomfortable situations. Clark opened their wounds in front of all her friends to see. Well, they would see the healing too. Faith found the some-thing that had been missing for the past six months. She had to forgive. First, she had to forgive Clark for telling her the truth as he saw it. The pain from his injuries contributed to the harsh reality. If he hadn't ended up in a hospital bed for over a month, he might have presented his argument differently. The sad thing was they would never know. Clark and Faith couldn't go back and change the colors of the past. They could only forge new paths for their futures.

Since leaving Castle Hill, Faith had gained a world of confidence. People in Paradise Hills valued her opinion. When Holly asked Faith to be a bridesmaid, they only knew each other for three months. "You are better at this than me. I need you," Holly had said. She valued Faith's advice. At home, Faith had to fight her mother to agree to go with the venue Clark wanted. The venue they never got to use. In Castle Hill, Faith was a figure people used to press for their own desires.

If Clark hadn't changed the course of their lives, Faith would have been a different person. Even though it came about in a way Clark hadn't intended, he had a significant role in making Faith the confident person she had become. To stay angry with him would have been the equivalent of wishing for a life Faith no longer wanted. Moreover, Clark had to deal with the fallout of their breakup. It probably was worse when his family realized they had cut her off because of the miscommunication on his part.

Faith forgave Clark for the hurt he never intended to inflict. She forgave herself for avoiding the fallout. Under the weight of her decision, Faith drew out a sigh. There was a difference between forgiving and forgetting. She would release herself and Clark from the burden of their mistakes. For as long as Faith lived, she would use it as a reminder to keep her distance. She exhaled from the weight of her decision and said, "Thank you for sharing this with me. You were right. It gives us the closure we needed."

6

AS EFFECTIVE AS SURPRISING A CAT

A slight chill in the air offset the warmth making the summer night comfortable. With the light glowing from the window on the left side of the house, it was like Faith's house was winking at them. It was late, and they should have headed home. Time with people who cared had a more powerful pull than the alarm clock that promised to rouse Clark in six more hours.

Faith's brother, Matthew, gave Clark the inside information over an online treasure hunter game. "Reel her in slowly," Matthew suggested. He ironically said it as he threw a bomb in the room. "Mom tried the straightforward approach." The debris from the explosion caused in their online game cleared to show an opening created on the other side of the room.

"That didn't end well." Clark meeting Faith on a blind date was as effective as her brother's video game-playing strategy. He got into the room but also destroyed the treasure he sought.

"We should have rethought how to approach that situation." Liam patted Clark on the shoulder.

"What did you expect?" Holly shook her head. She tapped

Liam with the back of her hand. "I still cannot believe you didn't tell me they were engaged."

"One, Faith wasn't supposed to get there early. Faith is always late when she doesn't want to do something. The plan was for Faith to see all of us there so she wouldn't have been completely blindsided." Liam held out his second finger. "It gave you plausible deniability."

Liam and Clark hatched the plan at the gym the week before. Clark wanted to approach Holly at her job. He passed by her kiosk a couple of times a day. Every time, Faith was busy with a customer, or one of the other girls was at the stand. Clark had hoped to reconnect with Faith gradually.

All things considered, it was the best they could do given the circumstances. If Clark had his way, he would have whisked Faith away to someplace romantic and convinced her they belonged together. That was considered kidnapping in all fifty states, so he had to go with Liam's idea. Liam's confident, "Get Faith to see that you have fun together. It worked for Holly and me. I proposed a week later," sounded plausible.

At this point, everyone except for Faith was in front of Holly and Liam's pickup and had formed a small circle.

"It made you look like a jerk," Kellen pointed at Liam with his pointer finger. He gestured with his thumb to Clark. "That was as effective as surprising a cat with a cucumber."

Only Kellen could refer to a viral video, and people would understand what he meant. In person, Kellen was abrupt and matter-of-fact. His social media feed, full of funny or heartwarming cat and dog videos, gave away Kellen's secret. The man willing to put his life on the line at any given moment was a softy on the inside. His latest share was of people who placed cucumbers in front of unaware cats. When the cat saw the cucumber, it hissed, jumped, and skittered away. Faith hadn't hissed, but she had followed all the other reactions.

Once upon a time, Clark's instinct worked to his advantage. He always found the best fishing spots. Within days of going out on a hunting trip, he'd have an elk large enough to fill half a freezer. "My instinct failed me," he admitted. "I thought Faith blocked me because she was in love with me." He shrugged, "and once I explained why I reacted the way I had, she'd find it in her heart to give me a second chance."

"By taking her on a virtual shooting excursion." Misha grimaced.

Clark didn't know how to feel about Faith's friend. Mischa's mouth made up for her diminutive stature. While Clark appreciated that Mischa said what she meant, he didn't like that it was the disapproval of him as a person. Mischa was Faith's friend. Friends could make or break a relationship. They either sowed seeds of support or dropped lines to break connections.

"She's a good shot," Clark replied. "I picked a game she could win. This way, Faith would feel like she had the upper hand at something."

Mischa blinked as though Clark had fed her information she hadn't previously known. "So, men let women win games?" She regarded Kellen with the corner of her eyes and frowned. Kellen looked up at the stars like he was searching for a constellation.

"No," Clark lied to get his friend out of trouble. "We don't let them win. She's a better shot than me."

FAITH HAD LOST a lot on account of Clark. It turned out she gained as much in Paradise Hills. How many people had friends that would interrogate an ex-fiancé to determine his motives?

Clark appreciated the friends he grew up with. They taught him the value of relationships. However, none had called him to task for how he treated Faith.

At first, they offered support. They delivered food trays to the house so his mother could spend as much time at the hospital. His mother asked the questions and tracked the medications, physical therapy sessions, and nurses' rotations. Nobody learned of the breakup until Faith sent out the cancellation letters.

Then the rumors began. They decided Clark got into the accident because he had a secret girlfriend. The next logical explanation was Faith found out; They argued; Then, she left town to leave the girlfriend to take care of him. Not one of them talked to him the way Kellen or Mischa had.

"It's getting late," Clark glanced at the house. He tried and failed to win Faith's favor. He'd find other opportunities to make things right. They had been out too late, and he was too tired to figure out the how and when.

Liam cast him an apologetic glance. "I'm sorry it didn't work out how you wanted." He wrapped his arm around Holly's shoulder to guide her to the passenger side of his pickup.

"I appreciate the help," Clark dug in his pocket for his keys.

He noticed Kellen and Mischa remained in place and regarded him with a suspicious eye. Clark couldn't blame them. He had been in town for less than a month and ruffled Faith's feathers. They were beautiful feathers too. "Goodnight, you two." Kellen waved and headed to his pickup with Mischa.

Clark stole a glance at Faith's window. He had lost more than a future. He lost his past. Faith had been his friend for as long as Clark could remember. Before they dated, she cheered

Paradise Hills Summer

for him when he got the touchdown and told him when the success got to his head. What Faith said mattered. She had a way of telling Clark the truth that forced him to focus on the benefit of hearing it.

When they were in classes together, teachers sat them together. Her presence settled him. Clark loved Faith. If there was one thing he learned from their time apart, it was Clark needed Faith more than she needed him.

7

MOVING ON

*D*ressed in her favorite pink plaid leggings and long-waisted t-shirt, Faith curled up against the back corner of her couch. She was getting ready to call her mother. Something told Faith it would be a long talk, so she might as well make sure she was comfortable.

When Faith left Castle Hill, she wasn't on the best of terms with her mother. Everyone thought Faith was the bridezilla. When in fact, it was her mother who grew overbearing and acted outright ugly over the wedding that never happened.

Hope Alexander declared that since it was the only wedding she was going to plan for her daughter, it had to be perfect. Faith wasn't the type of person who liked to make herself look good by showing other people's faults, so she did her best to hide how horribly her mother behaved.

As the timeline progressed, the situation strained the mother-daughter relationship to the near breaking point.

Then Clark broke up with Faith. At first, her mother raged with indignity. However, as the days passed and Faith faded into the abyss of grief, Hope Alexander came to terms with what had happened. Her attempt to make something special

Paradise Hills Summer

for Faith created an even bigger problem, and her commanding voice softened to take on a contrite tone.

With tears in her eyes, she implored Faith to, "Let me go talk to Clark and his mother."

Neither Clark nor his mother answered Hope's call.

The recent revelation of Clark's note was a gift to Faith. She could release her residual baggage. There was nothing she could have done to prevent the breakup. Clark had second thoughts and created an impassable test. For all Faith knew, the hidden note could have been a Freudian slip.

Faith's mother picked up the call on the first ring. She didn't wait for Faith to greet her. "Hi, honey. It's good to hear from you."

Faith didn't know how to begin, so she blurted it out. "I saw Clark yesterday?"

There was a brief moment of silence. Then her mother asked, "How did it go?"

From there, Faith retold the story without the feelings. Her mother didn't need to know the ups and downs that had Faith emotionally exhausted. Faith wished a letter could fix the broken situation. As soon as Faith finished the story, her mother repeated the story to Faith's father, John. She returned to the conversation to say, "I'll call you right back, sweetie."

Within minutes via a group chat, her father explained how he texted her brother Matthew while they were talking. Since Matthew was the techie of the Alexander family, he initiated a group Google Hangouts call. Her parents were in one square at the bottom of her phone, and her brother was in a mini-screen beside them. Faith guessed by the clenched lips and forced smiles that a "family discussion" had taken place before she was added to the call.

"What are the odds of you two being set up on a blind date?" her mother marveled. "Maybe this is a sign."

Her mother's enthusiastic response contrasted the point she emphasized throughout Faith's engagement with Clark. Back then, Hope Alexander drove the point that effort led to happiness. Her mother's motto was, "If you leave anything to chance, you're setting yourself up for a fiasco." Hope's declaration of a random coincidence preceding a life change triggered a range of warning flares in the back of Faith's mind.

Her brother, Matthew, piped into the conversation. "Does this mean I can go back to playing Madden with Clark?"

Faith didn't want her brother to choose sides, but he could have thrown out some indignation on Faith's behalf. Something like, "The nerve of the guy showing up six months later and acting like he hadn't caused a minor civil war in Castle Hill."

Then again, Matthew's reaction was consistent. When Faith explained the cancellation of the wedding, her brother mourned the loss of a gaming partner.

Friendships ran deep in their small town. The loss of a friend was the equivalent of losing a limb. Faith didn't know it then, but it was becoming more apparent that her only brother considered Clark a major organ.

Her growing suspicion prompted Faith to ask, "Is there something you want to tell me?"

When Matthew scratched at his goatee, Faith's stomach sank. Her ex-fiancé was inadvertently a member of her small group of friends. Bit by bit, she saw that he had a close relationship with her family, as well.

"I may have been playing online with Clark," Matthew's eyes darted to the side of the screen. "But we haven't done anything together in real life."

Faith shook her head. This wasn't how things were supposed to turn out. Her brother shouldn't have to choose

Paradise Hills Summer

sides in a relationship. She pushed aside the sting of betrayal. "I hope you whooped him."

Matthew smiled contritely. "If it makes you feel better, we talked about you a lot."

It didn't make her feel better. The knot tightened in her stomach. What had Matthew divulged to Clark during their video game battles? She made a conscious effort not to talk about Clark. But that didn't mean her brother hadn't picked up clues from what she failed to mention.

"While we are telling the truth, I might as well contribute to the discussion," the confidence in her mother's voice wavered. "About two months ago, Betsy and I picked up our weekly bridge game. A while back, she mentioned Clark was moving to Paradise Hills. She asked us not to say anything. We talked and agreed that we should never have had our fingers in your relationship in the first place."

Not much had changed. Faith's mother still had an agenda. Irritation tightened in Faith's spine. She bet Betsy didn't want Faith to know Clark lived in Paradise Hills because she worried that Faith would try to connect with her Clark.

Her father, who had been silent for the duration of the call, nodded his agreement with what Faith's mother said.

Faith laughed at Mischa's theory. Her discussion with her parents proved Mischa may have been closer to the truth than either of them realized. Clark had a purpose, and somehow Faith was a piece of it. Moreover, her parents hadn't spoken with Faith about Clark, but nobody shared that they hadn't spoken with Clark about Faith. What secrets were they keeping, and how would it affect Faith's new life?

Faith hoped her mother would say something to calm the rocking sensation that had Faith's heart beating out of sync. Their explanation of how Clark could keep tabs on her while she was out trying to forget him did the opposite. She thought

37

it was best to wrap up the call. If Faith stayed on the phone with her family for much longer, she would say something she'd regret later. Then it would get back to Clark. She faked a yawn. "It's getting late. I should go."

"Wait. What did you tell him?" Her mother didn't want to involve herself in their relationship but sure was eager to hear what had transpired.

She was back at square one. Obviously, Clark walked into the situation armed with information from her family. First, they, or her mother specifically, were too blunt with sharing information. Then her mother went to the other extreme and held her tongue because she didn't want to interfere. Was it too much to ask people to land somewhere in the middle of sharing the truth?

For the past six months, whether they intended to or not, her family's silence on the topic of Clark's family confirmed Faith's wariness. She was oblivious to anything that had to do with love. It frustrated Faith. How could she be so on target when it came to business yet blunder in matters of the heart?

Faith pursed her lips in determination. Time would reveal what she needed to do to assert herself. Until then, she'd reside in the calm she developed through the hours spent with Skye.

A thin line creased her mother's brow. "My foolishness caused this." Her mother's confession softened the blow of disappointment. For months before Clark's blow-up, Faith walked the tenuous line between blushing bride and damsel on the verge of being consumed by a momzilla.

"You weren't the only one who made bad choices," The sympathy Faith's father offered didn't excuse the actions. Faith admired how her father recognized fallibility but still loved the person. He addressed Faith, "Don't think too hard, honey. The answer is right in front of you."

In a sentence, Faith's father summed up what Faith lacked. Faith couldn't see the solution. She only saw the pieces that created the mammoth, sized problem. Faith wanted a life where she could be confident with her decisions. Yet, every time she committed to a decision, it came back to haunt her.

FAITH ALMOST DROPPED a large iced green tea with mint when she looked up and saw Clark standing in line at her coffee kiosk. When she tried to recover, she grasped the cup too tightly. The clear plastic cup buckled, then the lid popped off, and the contents poured down the front of Faith's red apron. Faith gasped as the chill traveled from her chest to her belly. "I am sorry." She rushed to make a replacement drink for the woman on the other side of the counter.

The woman, who was old enough to be Faith's grandmother, dressed in a linen tunic and loose-fitting pants, looked like she had recently been in a yoga class. Her face held an uninterpretable serenity. She glanced quickly at Clark and leaned forward before whispering, "I would have done the same thing. I'm glad it was you and not me." She winked and left Faith to stand there in slacked jaw shock.

After that, Faith made it a habit to keep an eye out for any tall, dark-haired, muscular men heading in her direction. It surprised her how many passed by her kiosk throughout the day. At first, she thought Clark's return clouded her mind. Instead, he opened her eyes to what she had been missing all along.

One particularly handsome man passed by wearing a dress shirt and a tie. The shirt, tight against his arms, was loose around his waist. Faith craned her neck to watch him pass by. "Where did he come from, and are there more like him?" Why she asked made little sense. It wasn't like Faith would talk to the man. She was still gun-shy. Until she understood the matters of the heart, all men were off limits.

Misty's voice conveyed admiration for the subject of Faith's comment. "Our head barista has returned to the land of the living."

Faith had to chuckle at her friend's comment. It seemed that Clark's explanation of what went wrong in the past had cleared the clouds in Faith's mind. One day she'd thank him.

She blinked herself back to reality. They were at work and had things to accomplish. Faith's eyes fell on Clark, standing on the other side of the counter. His lips were pressed flat, and the vein in his neck twitched. Faith's face reddened at having been caught gawking at a man. She kept confined to a safe zone, and the first time she tested the waters of single-hood, she got caught.

Misty bumped into Faith. She pressed into the counter and set her hand on her chest. "How does that song go? It's raining men." Faith loved Misty's spunky personality. More than once, she coaxed a smile out of a cranky customer. Misty had a knack for saying the right thing to add levity to tense situations.

Clark shook his head at Misty's joke, and his grin broadened, proving that Misty's flirtation worked. His smile was a punch in Faith's stomach.

As quickly as the sensation hit, Faith took inventory of the situation. Why did it matter to her if he liked Misty? She had no claim on Clark. By finding Faith and telling her what happened, Clark had made peace with her. It was only fair for Faith to let him move on with his life.

She stepped aside to make room so Misty had full access to Clark. Or at least as much access when a fake marble, Formica

Paradise Hills Summer

counter separated them. "You take his order. I'll make his drink."

Misty's lips widened into a full grin. "What can I get for you, handsome?"

"I'll have an iced green tea with mint," was the last thing Faith heard. Once she knew what Clark wanted, there wasn't any point in her being a part of the conversation.

While she scooped ice into the cup, she remembered the hotel had asked her to make a tray. Liam and Holly were meeting with management to review security measures for their wedding. Faith wanted to make sure soft sugar cookies were added to the platter for Holly. With the next item on her agenda in place, Faith set Clark's drink on the counter and left him and Misty to get more acquainted.

8

EXIT INTERVIEW

The bright, warm weather brought a lull in business, giving Faith plenty of time to think about her parents and Clark. Her parents were good people who tried to make their small town a place people would be proud to call home. Her mother and father ran a feed store for ranchers. They happily worked long hours because they knew what they did mattered.

As a messy-haired, mild-mannered boy, Clark worked hard at whatever he set his mind to. It was what attracted Faith to him. When they were in school, Clark wasn't like the other kids who said what they learned didn't apply to their world. He set his mind to learning everything the teachers set in front of him. Even when he was a kid, everyone realized Clark Grayson would excel at whatever he endeavored to accomplish.

Faith was just as motivated. However, she didn't shine as brightly as Clark. They partnered her with him, so he could help her. She learned the material and passed the tests. Behind the scenes, teachers gave Faith kudos. Clark won the public accolades. The move to Paradise Hills brought the first notions

Paradise Hills Summer

of recognition for Faith. At Castle Hill, she was an accessory. In Paradise Hills, Faith mattered.

Her mind drifted back to Castle Hill. What had Clark and her family talked about over the months? Who started the conversation that brought peace between the two families? Had the Alexanders and Graysons come to the truce because Faith wasn't there to mar the family alliances? She sighed. Why did she think of the questions long after everyone else had left the conversation? If she went back and asked anyone, she'd come across as argumentative. The last time Faith confronted conflict, it burned her. She wasn't about to make that mistake again.

Faith tried pushing the situation out of her mind. Then, her father posted pictures of a fishing trip. Clark's father and three other men stood beside him. All the men wore fishing vests with lures attached to the pockets. They held up the fish they had caught that day. It was like her call home had given her father permission to be truthful about the reconciliation with the Grayson family. Faith hoped it was a coincidence and not that her father hid the friendship until they had talked.

Faith was sitting on a stool by the register and waiting for the last couple minutes of her shift when Clark approached the counter. Faith straightened her posture to appear professional. "What can I get for you?"

Clark seemed relaxed. It was obvious to her that he was at the end of his day. "Are you doing anything after work?"

Faith searched the surrounding area. Misty had left for the day. So, there was nobody to distract Clark. "I hadn't planned anything." She wished she had plans. Not that Faith wanted Clark to be jealous. But as the story of them unfolded, the confidence Faith had developed weakened. Already, Clark knew she had to be set up on a blind date. Her parents

43

couldn't tell her the truth about life at home. From the outside looking in, she probably looked pathetic.

Nothing important sounding came to mind, so she went with the truth. "I don't have any plans."

A grin flashed and faded from Clark's face. He wore a polo shirt and sheer athletic pants. As best as Faith could tell, Clark had no pressing appointments either. "Would you mind meeting up with me when you're done?" Before Faith had time to reject his request, Clark added, "I just wanted to ask you a couple of questions. It shouldn't take too much time."

She pretended to brush away a crumb. "Is it something we can discuss now?"

Clark scanned the lobby area. Faith's eyes followed to see what he was looking for. People were too focused on their activities to pay Faith and Clark any mind.

"I'd prefer we discuss this in private." Clark seemed a little nervous.

Prickles of tension gripped Faith. "Is something wrong?" She heard about couples breaking up and one suing the other for financial fees incurred during a relationship. Was Clark going to ask her to pay for the cost of the ring or, even worse, for causing the accident?

"No, nothing to worry about. I'd offer to buy you a cup of coffee." Clark gestured at the coffee kiosk. His hand rose to pull at his ear. "How about some ice cream? I know a place that makes a mean butter pecan."

The image of the place he hinted at came to Faith. Jenny's Ice Cream Shop made the best of every flavor of ice cream. Faith checked her step tracker to discover that it was time for her to close the kiosk. She only needed to clean the last of the coffee pots and wipe down the counters. "Is it okay if I meet you there in a half hour?"

When his shoulders dropped, Faith saw the tension she

Paradise Hills Summer

hadn't noticed previously fall away. It hadn't occurred to her that Clark may have worried about her declining his offer. Seeing that she brought him happiness sent a jolt of delight through her. As soon as Faith associated the sensation with Clark, she tightened to make it stop. She and Clark were not together. Faith reminded herself that it didn't matter if she made him happy.

"See you there." Clark tapped the counter and waved his goodbye.

Once he was out of her field of vision, a tremor of uncertainty struck Faith's core making it difficult for her to focus. She missed the sink when she disposed the coffee and couldn't figure out where she put the mop. Her miscues were so ridiculous, Faith whispered to herself, "Pull it together." When that didn't work, she replayed the last conversations with his family. They didn't want her anywhere near Clark. The reconciliations that took place in Faith's absence added salt to the wound. Her mother said otherwise, but Faith put two and two together and concluded that they mended the broken bonds because she wasn't there.

The humbling Faith gave herself was enough for her to remain clear-headed. However, she found she had been too effective because seeing Clark added to her anxiety. Faith began to fear he would assert what she already knew and asked for the meeting to set a clear boundary. She didn't want to relive the scene at the hospital again.

By the time Faith reached the door to the ice cream shop, she had a stomachache that made it impossible for her to think about wanting a sample. She inhaled a breath, opened the door, and braced herself for what would greet her on the other side.

A waft of cool air surrounded her, and Faith wished she had brought a sweater. Part of her knew she was looking for an excuse to avoid the situation. *It's too late to back out now.* And like that, the inner strength she developed over the six months returned. Things weren't as bad as they could have been. Refreshed from the new insight, Faith stepped into the ice cream parlor and moved before the closing door crashed into her backside.

The ice cream parlor had black and white ceramic tiles on the floor. A row of tables topped with white Formica was opposite the ice cream counter. Clark rose from his seat at the table furthest back in the parlor. He smiled sweetly and encouraged Faith to join him with a tilt of his head.

Faith swallowed the lump in the back of her throat and returned the smile. If they were together, she would have allowed herself to hurry. But they weren't, so Faith forced herself to walk at a casual pace toward him.

Clark moved to the chair across from where he was sitting and rested his hand on the back of it. When Faith reached the table, he pulled it out for her to sit. She smiled and thanked him. As she sat, her nose caught a whiff of his cologne. The fragrance brought an ocean of memories. All of them were pleasant and filled Faith with an angst to go back and relive them. She blinked quickly to control the onslaught of images. By the time Clark sat across from Faith, she was thankful to have regained her composure.

"So, how was your day?" Clark held his hands folded in front of him.

"It was good. How do you like your new job?" When Faith left Castle Hill, Clark worked as a maintenance engineer. His job as a personal trainer was a career change Faith would never have been able to predict.

"I'm doing well. I think it's easier for people to relate to me." He blushed, "Because I started as an unhealthy person,

Paradise Hills Summer

I'm real about what it takes to make changes. People seem to appreciate that."

The way Clark said it made sense to Faith. A server dressed in a long white apron that hid his shorts and t-shirt brought two dishes of ice cream to the table. He set a scoop of vanilla ice cream with nuts in front of Clark and two scoops of butter pecan ice cream in front of Faith.

Faith wrinkled her brow in confusion. "I didn't order."

Clark repositioned his bowl. "I worried you'd be shy, so I ordered for you."

"I'm not shy," Faith objected. She was a little put out that Clark assumed she would be.

"You hardly ate your soup the other night." Clark positioned his spoon to dig into the bowl of ice cream

She quickly replied, "Because I had a stomachache."

Clark arched his eyebrow. "How is your stomach today?"

"Fine," Faith snapped.

"Good." He gave a swift nod. "Then you won't have any problems eating your ice cream."

Faith's mouth fell open. She couldn't think of a retort, so she shut it.

The grin on Clark's face said it all. Clark one-Faith zero. He had always been competitive. His smile flattened, and he took on a serious expression. "I wanted to ask if there was anything you could change about me, what would it be?"

Faith choked on the bite of ice cream she had eaten. She coughed hard enough for the server to hurry to the table with a glass of water. After a gulp that was large enough for her to down half the glass, she cleared her throat. "I don't understand the question?"

Clark explained, "You just left. There was no goodbye. We didn't have any of the conversations where we discussed what we didn't get from the relationship."

Disappointment washed over Faith and dripped like a surprise rain surge. Clark had set her up. He wanted to finish what he had started all those months ago. Even worse, he did it with her favorite ice cream. There was no way Faith would ever be able to eat it again without associating it with him telling her how bad she was. She stammered as she tried to find something to say. "I don't know what to tell you. Other than how things ended…I didn't have any complaints."

Faith braced herself for Clark to take his turn at her. He would tell her it was because she turned into a different person when they were engaged. It wasn't the wedding that changed her. It was having to buffer Clark from Faith's mother's demands that altered her personality. Clark wanted to have a say in the wedding arrangements. Her mother dismissed the idea. Faith then had to go to battle with either Clark or her mother. Even when she won, she lost.

"I'm sorry about that." Clark sounded sincere.

Faith shrugged. "Well, it's behind us now. It isn't like we can do anything about it."

"No, it isn't." He looked at her through the top of his eyes. "Your parents believe I'm the reason why you won't go home."

It became clear to Faith. He was there at her parent's request. Not because he wanted to make things right with her. "I don't go home because I'm busy," she lied. Clark didn't need to know that she didn't want to go home because her mother contributed to the demise of her happily ever after. Or, that the chaos of their breakup alienated her from her hometown. "When things settle down, I'll go back."

Clark grinned. "Like for your birthday?"

Faith did some quick math. Her birthday was in a month. "I can't make any promises."

Paradise Hills Summer

"What about your mother's birthday?" He quirked his brow.

"I'll be there for that." Faith had two months to mentally prepare for her visit to Castle Hill.

The quirked expression changed to one that promised to assess Faith's reaction. "She's planning a party."

Of course, her mother was planning a party. She liked to celebrate in a big way. Thoughts of the guest list gave Faith heart palpitations. She'd have to face half the town.

"If it would make you feel better, I'd go with you." His eyes searched her face.

The caution in his eyes threw Faith off kilter. He expected disappointment but made the offer anyway. It brought her back to when he offered to take her to the dance when Chris Brubaker couldn't. Her heart hitched. Was it possible she was wrong about Clark?

"What are the odds?" Mischa's voice was bright against the fog ushered in with the memories.

"Do you mind if we join you?" Kellen didn't wait for an answer. He took the seat beside Clark. "We thought we'd head out to the river. You're welcome to come."

Faith had never been so happy to see her friends. They bought her time. Time to come up with a way to help Clark come to terms with the past. Their families came together because Faith was out of the picture. The only way they'd remain friends was if she stayed away.

49

9

THE GROUP DATE

Faith hadn't given Clark much to work with at the ice cream shop. Clark expected anger. He expected her to tell him how his impulsivity ruined a good thing. It was something Faith had said frequently over the years. "Take it easy, Clark. Let's think through the situation before we make a final decision."

If he had presented the idea of an elopement before the wedding, she'd have given him a better idea of how to do it. But Clark was too excited by the idea of them having something special between them.

The pendulum of his disappointment went equally far, making him say things he regretted. He was prepared to convince Faith he would do whatever it took to win her back. But Clark never got to that point in the conversation.

Clark wanted things to be right between Faith and him.

Faith's friends had a different agenda.

They had to have developed a plan to run interference. As soon as Clark was on the cusp of connecting with Faith, they'd appear.

The night of the group date, he watched Faith walk into the

cafe. His heart raced like it was their first date. It sank just as quickly when he saw her do an about-face. Clark was about to go after Faith when Kellen and Mischa ran into her.

If he and Faith had had ten minutes alone, he could have asked for a fresh start.

Later, at her house, he tried to wait them out to get time alone with her. When Faith's head bobbed to fight off sleep, Clark knew his chance had passed. Even when she was at work, Misty ran between them. He was growing impatient. When would he get his chance to reconnect with Faith?

A caravan of friends driving to the river softened his frustrations. Summer was the season of beginnings. It was the time when seeds sprouted, love bloomed, and friends brought out the best in each other. Not much was better than a summer night in Montana.

Kellen stashed cords of wood in the back of his pickup, and Liam brought the ice chests, chairs, and blankets. They drove with the windows down and country music blaring from the radio. Mischa and Faith sat in the back seat and sang the songs in harmony.

Occasionally, there was a silence in the melody. Clark guessed they were talking and joking about the lyrics they sang. Summer in Montana meant friends and fun. His frustration gave way to the hope that he'd have a chance to get cozy with Faith.

They parked the pickups a couple of hundred feet from the bridge and walked the hundred feet to the riverbank. The trees extended high in the sky, creating a canvas that Clark couldn't help appreciating. He inhaled the scent of the wood warmed by the sun and the cool notes added by the water. It was as if the breeze took his worries and carried them someplace far, where he'd never be able to find them.

With the last bits of sunlight dancing on the horizon, the

women gathered rocks to make a ring around the fire, and the men piled the wood. They chatted about all sorts of things they'd never remember. What mattered was that they were there together, enjoying a summer night.

In a pause, Kellen scanned the area. The women were off in the distance. One was pointing, and the others were focused in that general direction. "Mischa gets so distracted. I bet she found something and is trying to convince the rest of them it's proof that aliens have been out here." The proud grin on Kellen's face contradicted the cynicism. It was obvious to everyone. Kellen adored Mischa. His eyes constantly followed her wherever she went. Clark knew by the soft expressions on their faces when they regarded each other that an engagement was forthcoming.

Watching them made Clark miss being with Faith. They always had so much fun together. Faith got his jokes. Even when they weren't funny, she'd laugh. First, she'd say something like, "I'll give that one a three for effort."

Then when Clark acted like he didn't know what she was talking about, Faith would laugh.

He'd laugh with her.

His heart pinched when he thought about how he had taken for granted how much fun it was to amuse her. His mother giggled at his antics, but it wasn't the same. What he would do to hear Faith laugh at his jokes again.

Clark smiled at Kellen's comment and returned to stacking the wood. "What's with you and Faith?" Kellen asked.

"What do you mean?" Clark asked. Wasn't it obvious? They had a history.

"The surprise introduction, then we find you in the middle of an intense moment at the ice cream shop. I can't figure out if you're someone we're supposed to support or someone we need to watch out for. Like, are we going to be featured on one of those true crime shows?"

CLARK CHUCKLED. Their hesitance to leave him alone with Faith made sense. Faith never mentioned being engaged. From what he'd heard from Liam, she hardly talked about Clark. Clark thought it would be better if he answered Kellen's question with an explanation of what happened. "I've known Faith for pretty much all of our lives. She's here because we'd never fought. Sure, we bickered. But in all the time we've known each other, whenever there was a problem, one of us would sit the other down and say, 'let's talk it out.' Our first fight was a doozy. Our parents got involved, and it became a big mess. A big enough mess for Faith to toss in the towel on all of us and skip town."

Kellen stood straight. "You moved from a town to resume a fight with an ex-girlfriend?"

"Fiancée," Clark corrected. "No, I didn't move all the way from Castle Hill to fight with Faith. I moved here because Liam helped me get a job managing the fitness center at the resort. Faith being here was a coincidence."

"What would you have done if you hadn't met her here?"

Clark held out his hand for Kellen to pass him a log. "Eventually, we'd have met up. Faith couldn't stay away from Castle Hill forever. Her family is there."

"Then, you would fight with her?"

"You get stuck on one topic," Clark set down the wood. The ground shifted under his feet as he made his way to Kellen. "Our friends and family controlled every aspect of our lives. Even though I was right, the way I went about handling things was wrong. I broke her heart. If that wasn't bad enough, our families proved the point I was trying to make when they broke her spirit."

He drifted back to the past. It was shock added to shock. Since Kellen had heard about the letter, Clark started from there. "I thought for sure Faith would be at the courthouse. I waited on the bench outside the building. Ten minutes turned to twenty. I called her. She didn't pick up."

By now, Kellen was standing beside him to hear the full story.

"Twenty turned to thirty. I had my answer. Faith wasn't coming. So, I took my pickup and drove down the two-lane highway. I had no plan of where to go. It just had to be as far away from Castle Hill as possible."

Kellen's eyes wandered toward the women, and Clark's followed. They were skipping rocks. Faith pulled her arm back and flicked her wrist perfectly. The rock skipped five times. The glow from the sunset reflected off the water. His body tilted. Clark could tell Kellen was torn between joining the women and hearing the rest of the story. "She left because you left?"

"No. She called two hours later. If I could go back in time, I wouldn't have picked up the call. Then I'd have had time to cool off. But I picked up the call. I told her I didn't want to be a part of her horse and pony show and called off the wedding."

"Whoa," Kellen's voice lowered. "That was your first fight?"

"Then I rolled my pickup. My parents thought it was her fault. It just went downhill from there." Clark's anger convinced him it was Faith's fault he was in the hospital. He never wanted to see Faith again. If she loved him, she would have been at the courthouse, and the crash wouldn't have

Paradise Hills Summer

happened. After Faith's first visit to the hospital, his parents, having heard only Clark's side of the story, enforced his request.

Kellen scratched the back of his head and rested his hands on his waist. "I don't know, dude."

Clark mirrored Kellen's posture and positioned his hands on his waist too. "I thought so too. But what are the odds we'd move to the same town and join the same social circle? I'd never introduced Liam to Faith. It was Liam's idea I meet their single friend. When Liam said the woman's name was Faith, I couldn't believe it. What are the odds of being set up on a blind date with the woman I intended to marry? If that isn't a sign that we were meant to be together, I don't know what to tell you."

Clark must have said the right thing because Kellen's head jerked, and he asked, "What did you say?"

"For some people, love is a surprise. Not me." Clark shook his head. "Love has been guiding me since we were kids. Before I knew what to do about it, I knew we would be together. The detours weren't in the picture, but that doesn't change the end of the story. Faith loved me enough to promise to spend her life with me. I need to remind her why she made the promise."

Liam and his brother, Mark, approached with matches and a handful of kindling. Before they got to the woodpile, Kellen assessed Clark with his eyes. They said that Clark hadn't fully gained his support, but he'd give him the space he needed to move forward with Faith. Clark tipped his head forward to acknowledge the agreement. He'd prove he was there for noble reasons.

Mark struck the match and cupped his hands over the kindling to give the fire a safe place to grow. The flames crawled along the thinner pieces of wood until they formed orange spires that threw sparks of yellow into the night air. The logs in the middle caught fire and burned with slow licks of yellow and blue beneath the orange.

Watching Liam and Mark bask in the glow of what they created struck a familiar chord in Clark. He missed his brothers. They were older and had moved to other towns. After what he went through with Faith, he understood why. On this night, like many others before it, Clark wondered if he'd have handled things differently if his brothers were there to talk to when he had concerns about being married. Rather than belabor what he didn't have, Clark focused on what was in front of him. He had a chance to get back his Faith.

The warmth of the flame compensated for the chill of the night air. The undulations of warm and cold brought an appreciation of both sensations. Clark couldn't put his finger on the moment. He just sensed that tonight was different. He surveyed the night around them until his eyes landed on the other side of the fire. Faith and Holly's sister, Madison, sat in chairs beside each other. They had their heads inclined toward each other and talked. The glow of the fire added a softness to Faith's cheeks. Clark inhaled. She was so beautiful. He didn't deserve her. But that didn't stop him from wanting her.

Clark shoved his hands in his pockets and roamed around the fire. Faith's eyes flitted toward him and back to Madison. He walked around to the other side of Faith and bent at his waist to get down to her level. "Can I get you something?"

Faith regarded him with a tender expression. "Ah, no, thank you."

"Let me do something nice for you, please." The path to gaining her forgiveness entailed many steps. Clark had to start at one. His heart implored Faith to say yes.

She thought for a moment, but it seemed like an eternity to

Clark. Would she accept his olive branch or give him the rejection he deserved? "I'll have water."

It was a small victory, but it was a victory, nonetheless. Clark grinned. "Madison, can I get you something?"

"No, I'm good for now." Her smile said she knew Clark was trying to gain good favor with Faith.

He nodded to Madison and addressed Faith, "I'll be back with the water."

When he returned with the water, Madison rose. "Here, you take my chair. I'll go sit with Mark."

"Are you sure?" Clark was not about to decline the opportunity to spend time with Faith, but he didn't want to push her away from her friends.

Madison flicked her hand to dismiss his concern. "I'm positive."

When she was a safe distance from the chair, Clark took his place beside Faith.

"It's been a while since we've been around a bonfire." The winter had been long and hard. The record-high snowfall combined with the emptiness from Faith's absence seemed unendurable. In those long months, Clark promised himself things would be different.

Faith's face twisted. Clark could tell she was trying to recall the last time they'd been to a bonfire. "Two summers ago. We had one at the lake. Remember the fishing trip where you found the huckleberry bushes."

Clark and Faith were the perfect couple back then. Whatever the situation, they worked well together. Clark caught and cleaned the fish. Faith brought a tool kit of spices, potatoes, and vegetables. Kind of like they were doing now, they sat around the fire after dinner with friends. He couldn't remember what they talked about. The feeling of being alive and never wanting the moment to end stuck with him. The edges of the sensation were there with him. It deepened when Clark saw Faith's facial features shift, and her eyes brightened with the recollection. There was a brief dropping of her guard, and just as quickly, the wall she erected to protect herself returned. Still, Clark saw it. He was on the verge of making things right with Faith.

10

PAINT PARTY

Mischa grumbled, "You know most people have fancy drinks and food when they celebrate with their bridal party."

"You're just upset because this isn't your super talent," Faith joked.

Mischa dipped her paintbrush into the paint container and slid it along the back of the park bench. While Faith could understand Mischa's sentiment, she didn't mind spending a Saturday afternoon on a community project.

Part of the appeal of Paradise Hills came from people in the community taking efforts to keep it beautiful. Instead of the traditional bachelor and bachelorette party, Liam and Holly had a painting party. The groomsmen touched up old-style lights, and the bridesmaids repainted the park benches. The night prior, they scrubbed everything down in preparation for the day's activities.

Holly paired off with Rebecca, the owner of the salon where she worked. They were at the opposite end of the park. Faith and Mischa worked as a team. Faith didn't want to say anything, but she suspected it was because she was the most patient with Mischa's no-nonsense approach to problems. It reminded Faith of her grandmother, so she laughed off the salty comments.

Mischa painted the seat and the back of the benches with a water seal. Faith touched up the arms with hunter-green paint.

Three benches away, Holly's sister Madison was painting a replica of the town tree on the bench. Liam's brother, Mark, had broken rank by separating from the men and joining her.

All the Lane men were attractive in their own way. Mark, a math teacher, had a boyish quirk in his mannerisms. The way he fell over himself when he was around Madison endeared him to everyone.

Madison, who had been through a difficult divorce, timidly accepted his kindness. The combination of their personalities created a level of cuteness that was the equivalent of a basket of puppies or kittens. Nobody complained that they were the only two who looked like they were having fun. Instead, they basked in the joy Mark and Madison seemed to be having.

Mischa tilted her head in appreciation toward Mark and Madison. "When do you think they'll get married?"

"Hard to tell," Faith replied. She knelt on the ground to paint the claw-footed park bench leg.

Everyone knew if it were up to Mark, they would already be married. Madison, who had been treated poorly by her ex-husband, stalled at every sign of progression. It bothered Faith that a person who promised to love through thick and thin would break their partner with hateful comments before garnering the courage to leave them.

She thought about Clark. At least he had the decency to end things when he thought Faith wasn't suited to his needs. Remembering what Madison shared about how her ex-husband treated her made Faith shudder.

Paradise Hills Summer

"Okay, different question," Mischa went around to the back of the bench. "Do you think you and Clark will get back together?"

Faith nearly dropped her paintbrush on the ground. She caught it by the bristles with her hand. "I don't know why I bothered to get my nails manicured this week." Instead of answering the question, she focused on the scrap towels stacked on a table off to the side of the big tree. "I'll be right back."

"I'll join you. We can use a break." Mischa came up alongside Faith. They both assessed the bench. They had finished anyway and could move on to another one.

Yes, she and Clark had been spending time together, but not much had happened between them. He'd stop by after work, and they'd go for a bite to eat. Sometimes they'd go for a ride down a country road and sit in the back of his pickup and talk for hours. Those lazy summer nights brought reminders of the things Faith loved about Clark. But she wasn't going to allow love to weaken her this time, and she certainly wasn't going to let her friends know that Clark had found the only soft place in her heart.

Faith took in the sights around the park while she meandered toward the table. People who weren't part of the bridal party joined in the activity. It was one thing she loved about Paradise Hills. People liked to pitch in and help. At this rate, they'd finish in under an hour.

"I caught that." Mischa gestured with her thumb toward the bench.

"What?" Faith watched Madison's daughters run in circles to try to catch Mark's sons. One boy took cover behind a tree. The other slowed down enough for Madison's oldest daughter to catch up to him. Right before she could tag him, he'd arch his back and pick up the pace. It was a game men still played.

61

"It's obvious Clark still has feelings for you," Mischa pressed. "When are you going to admit you're still in love with him?"

If the question had come from her parents or one of her friends from home, it would have made sense. Mischa was the one who identified Clark as the kidnapper, serial killer.

It had since been established that Liam had talked Clark into moving to Paradise Hills. The two had been friends for years and reconnected when Liam visited Clark. In a show of support, Liam worked out with Clark. From there, Clark helped Liam move beyond a month-long plateau. One thing led to another, and the two friends worked with the resort to expand the gym. The plan included having Liam inviting people who needed to train for movies to the resort. When they got there, Clark would work with them.

"Why do you taunt me?" Faith spoke with a Russian accent to add levity to the moment.

Mischa giggled. "I don't make fun of people. That's not my style. I'm more of a tell-the-truth when I should hold my opinion person."

Considering how Clark avoided Mischa like she was a seven-year-old with a cold, Faith could appreciate that Mischa was her friend. "You keep on being honest. At least I know where I stand with you."

"At least I'll have one friend when I'm old and honest," Mischa exhaled. "Just so you know, I approve."

"Approve of?" Faith thought it odd that Mischa would approve the enduring friendship.

"If you and Clark should get back together, I would approve." Mischa said it like it should have been obvious for Faith to follow the change in topic.

Not only had the change in topic confused Faith, but the

Paradise Hills Summer

change in Mischa's opinion of Clark also threw Faith through a conversational loop de loop. "How did he go from the kidnapper, serial killer to...."

"Can we just forget that whole incident," Mischa held out a container of wet wipes and a towel for Faith.

"If we can agree to avoid talking about Clark and me getting back together, you have a deal."

"Ooh," Mischa grimaced. "That's a hard deal."

"What's a hard deal?" Kellen, who was behind Mischa, set his hand on her shoulder and rubbed it. Clark was a couple of steps behind him.

Mischa's mouth fell open. Her widened eyes asked the same question that Faith feared voicing. Had Clark and Kellen overheard their conversation?

Faith handed Kellen the container of wipes. "Ah," She heard an odd-sounding laugh. Her eyes flitted to the area around them to see who made the noise. Then she realized it was her. She did it again, but it was louder.

Mischa slapped herself on the forehead and laughed too. Something about the way Mischa reacted cracked up Faith, and both women laughed even harder. This time it was a genuine laugh of appreciation. Both women inhaled to calm down. It worked until their eyes connected, and they laughed again.

Kellen's face grew serious. "What is so funny?"

"It's nothing for you to worry about." Mischa patted his arm." We were talking about how I get myself into trouble for being too honest."

"Oh," Kellen replied. Mischa's answer seemed to be enough to appease his concerns. He pointed with his eyes from Clark to Faith. Clark had his eyes glued on Mischa as though he were expecting her to say something antagonistic.

63

Kellen cleared his throat. "Clark and I were talking about hanging out tomorrow afternoon."

"Oh, that sounds like fun," Mischa sobered. "I could try out one of my new recipes."

Faith tuned out the conversation and directed her attention toward Madison and Mark. Madison had finished painting her picture, and they were admiring her work. Mark's hand had settled on Madison's lower back, and he kissed her on the cheek. Madison has been burned, but she was still willing to take a chance on love. It was such a lovely thing to see, but Faith knew from experience, it was a hard gap to bridge.

The next thing Faith heard was Mischa clap. "Earth to Faith."

Faith twitched to refocus her attention. "Yes?"

"Would you want to join us for lunch tomorrow?"

Somehow Clark had cemented his relationship with the significant others of her friends. When they were in Castle Hill, Faith had fallen into the small community trap. Friends and family created situations for her and Clark to strengthen their connection.

Clark had seen through it. He saw that without friends, he and Faith didn't have a strong relationship. Faith may fall for something the first time, but she wasn't foolish enough to make the same mistake twice. There was no way she would have her friend's influence over her relationship.

Faith thought back to her routine when she didn't know too many people in Paradise Hills. Until she could look at Clark without the pangs of longing, especially when she was in a situation where people naturally coupled, Faith needed a plan. Then it dawned on her. She spent most of her time horseback riding around the resort. It was something she could do alone. It was a habit she would resume, beginning tomorrow.

Paradise Hills Summer

Over the months, Faith had rid herself of the pain of the breakup. Now she hoped the quiet ride on the prairie would help her forget she was in love with the man who had broken her heart.

11

TIME

*A*fter they posted wet paint signs on all the benches and the lampposts, the wedding party met at Liam's parent's house for a barbecue. "It's nothing fancy," Liam said. "We'll have some burgers, brats, and beer."

When they stepped onto the back patio, Liam rolled his eyes. "My mother does not understand that a small gathering is a barbecue with friends."

Liam's mother had a table lined with glass pitchers by the door. A small chalkboard set on an easel listed the contents of the pitcher behind it: water, water with cucumber, water with lemon, and lemonade. Off to the side, she set a steel tub full of ice and several varieties of beers and wine coolers. The tables around the pool area had red and white checkered cloths and flowers in the middle. One table had stacks of board games. Liam's mother had gone as far as setting up a corn hole game at one end of the yard. Clark chuckled. Apparently, he and Faith weren't the only ones with family members who went above and beyond the requests for wedding arrangements.

A woman with a stylish bob and circular glasses held up her hands and exclaimed, "Welcome to our house. I'm Stella.

Paradise Hills Summer

We haven't met." She tapped Clark's bicep and said, "That's quite the gun show you have going there."

"Mom," Liam groaned.

Stella turned to the woman beside her. "We are old enough to flirt with young guys and be considered harmless?"

The other woman rubbed her chin and arched her right eyebrow. "I think we need to look like grandmothers."

"Really?" Liam addressed Clark. "Ignore her."

Stella playfully nudged Liam with her elbow. "I'm not a good mother if I don't embarrass my son every once in a while." Her affect changed to reflect a motherly tone. "Welcome to our home. Liam has said so many nice things about you. It's nice to meet you," and then she was off mixing in with the small group of women standing in a circle by their backyard fountain.

Clark found Faith in a matter of seconds. She changed from the long sleeve t-shirt and sweats she had worn earlier into some capris and a long sleeve plaid shirt. He imagined them sitting in the back of his pickup and watching the sunset. If Clark played his cards right, he'd sneak away with Faith. Maybe, she'd let down her guard, and he'd kiss her.

Faith must have sensed Clark's attention because she looked up from the group and caught his eye. Clark was about to smile when he saw her grin shrink a little. She averted her attention back to the discussion in front of her.

"Give it time," Liam said, "She'll come around."

"This isn't about me," Clark replied. "You're the one who is about to get married."

"Yes, and everyone knows that love happens at weddings."

"I could be so lucky," Clark picked two lite beers out from the tub and handed one to Liam.

"I said some stupid things to Holly," Liam confessed. "My ego read the situation wrong. I accused her of stalking me."

Clark choked on his beer. His eyes alternated from Liam to Holly, who was in with the group of women, and back to Liam.

Liam pointed at the group of women with his beer. "How much do you want to bet they're talking about us?"

Faith clutched at her chest, and the women giggled at something. Clark couldn't help himself. Everything said to leave her alone. To give her time, and everything would fall into place. His heart wanted to speed up the timeline. "How are we going to find out?"

"Easy," Liam replied. "We go over there. If they stop talking, it was about us. If they act like we aren't there or pull us into the conversation, we were wrong."

Mischa left the group with two empty glasses. Clark guessed they were talking about the drinks. "Loser has to run a mile."

"Deal!" Liam sauntered toward the huddle of women. Clark quickly stepped to fall in line with him. When they were closer to the women, Liam said to Clark, "Watching you run will be fun."

Holly noticed the two men first. Her eyes connected with Liam. The corner of her lips curved, and she greeted him with a quick tip of her chin. She said something to the women in the crowd and stepped away to meet Liam.

All eyes turned to acknowledge the forthcoming change in the group dynamic. Holly's sister, Madison, held up her glass like she wanted to freshen her drink. By the time Clark reached where the women were standing, they left Faith to herself. She turned to the right and then the left as though she were looking for someone. When Clark reached her, she bit at the corner of her lip. "Mischa was supposed to be right back. I should go find her."

Paradise Hills Summer

Before Faith could run off, too, Clark grabbed the chance to talk with her. "Can you answer a question for me?"

Faith's eyebrow furrowed toward the middle of her forehead.

To ease the concern, Clark leaned forward and spoke in a low, conspiratorial tone, "Liam and I had a bet. If I win, he has to run a mile."

Faith craned her neck to see something behind Clark but remained silent, giving him permission to continue with his question.

"What were you talking about earlier?" Clark fiddled with the collar of his shirt.

Faith's cheeks pinked. The twinkle in her eye challenged him. "Are you sure you want to know?"

"Ah, man!" Clark wasn't a strong runner. His cardio wasn't up to par with his muscle strength. "Give it to me."

"I guess you're old enough to hear this." Faith cast her eyes to the area above his head and rushed her words. "We were trying to decide how many sticky bras we need." She squinted in what Clark presumed was anticipation of his laughter.

"That's it?" Clark couldn't believe his luck. "Sticky bras." He curled his hand in a fist and silently celebrated. It would be fun watching Liam run that mile.

"We don't want to have any wardrobe malfunctions," Faith explained.

Clark nodded quickly, "That makes sense."

Now that he had Faith to himself, he lost his words. They had been together for most of their life. It should have been easy to talk with her. The weight of wanting to reconnect fought with Clark's desire to give Faith the time to forgive him. The dilemma created a mental log jam. He shifted his weight from his heels to his toes and back again. Still, nothing came to mind.

69

Clark knew he had created the distance between them. For the life of him, he couldn't figure out what it would take to bridge the gap. He cleared his throat. "Can I ask you one more thing?"

"Sure," Faith gave the sweet grin Clark remembered from when they sat together on the rock all those years ago.

Clark hoped his next question would be the one to bring them back together. "What can I do?"

Her lip quirked. "What do you mean?"

"We had something special. I ruined it. What can I do to fix it? To get us back to where we were before I lost my cool."

Faith's lips parted as though she was ready to reply. Then she pursed them. Clark had seen her do it a million times before. She motioned to say something and thought it better to keep her reply to herself.

"Just go ahead and say it." Clark needed Faith to say some-thing–anything for him to work with.

She sighed, "I don't know what to say."

"Just tell me how you feel. You didn't say anything about the letter. You haven't said anything about how you've been since you left Castle Hill. Dang, you haven't told me where I could go." Clark had rehearsed the comebacks. If Faith told him where to go, he'd say only if you go with me. If she called him names, he'd agree.

Faith said, "I have to thank you. When we broke up, I thought it was the end of the world. My parents wouldn't let me fall apart." Her eyes traveled to someplace in the past and returned just as quickly. "We had to pay for the caterer, so we had a dinner, anyway."

Clark heard about it through the grapevine. His parents never mentioned it. Probably because they weren't invited. The friends had to choose sides. Some didn't get the luxury. They received a letter of explanation and an apology for the inconvenience the change in the plans caused. Clark and Faith

Paradise Hills Summer

were divorced before they were married. He nodded for her to continue. To get to the place where he could do something.

"At the time, I went through the motions. But after a while, I got the message. I had to like myself."

Faith wasn't saying anything that helped Clark. He loosened his shoulders to relieve the tension building.

She continued, "I think I need to apologize to you."

With that being the last thing Clark expected, he tilted his ear toward Faith. "I asked what I could do."

"Accept my apology." Faith fiddled with her fingers. "I made you feel like our friends and family were more important. Don't get me wrong. They were important, but not more than you. I failed before we started. But look at us now. We are on our own. None of the people who mattered then are here. Obviously, I could make it without them or their approval. I should have realized it sooner. I'm sorry."

Mischa approached Clark and Faith with two drinks in her hand. "Someone spiked the lemonade with Southern Comfort." She passed the drink in her right hand to Faith. Faith took a sip. The change in her facial expression communicated her approval.

Kellen and Liam's brother, Hunter, approached the group of three. "The game's on in the man cave."

"That's our sign." Mischa tugged at Faith's elbow, and they went off together. Faith followed without looking back. Clark watched her slip away, but this time was different. He had an idea of how to get her back.

12

DO IT AGAIN

Mischa held out her phone to show a woman wearing flesh-colored tape shaped like a butterfly. "This is what we have."

A tinge of sadness flushed through Faith. When Faith was the bride, she had mismatched dresses. Her bridesmaids had the choice of several styles of dresses to work with her color scheme. Things like bra size and hip measurement didn't matter. They got dresses that worked with their body style. Faith wanted everyone to feel good about her wedding. In the end, the only person that mattered had an issue with the wedding. But Clark said too little too late.

It was Holly's turn to have the perfect wedding, and Faith would do whatever she could to show her support, even if it meant wearing a dress that required a creative support system. Faith took the phone and scrolled to the screen. "This has four stars. I don't know." She pressed the button and read through the reviews. Several five-star reviews bragged about how they danced at proms and felt comfortable with the dresses.

Then Faith read a one-star review. "The tape came loose in

the middle of a wedding." She handed the phone to Mischa. "That would be me. I'll go back to the duct tape."

"Let me see." Mischa took back her phone. She scrunched her face. "It has twenty positive reviews and two poor reviews. You read the bad reviews?"

Faith grumbled, "If one person gets the defective bra, we all know it will be me. I have issues with things not sticking."

"Contrary to what our fathers have said," Mischa emphasized said. "Duct tape cannot fix everything."

A shadow appearing at the edge of Faith's peripheral vision caught her attention. Mischa must have noticed it at the same time. Both women looked up to find Kellen and Clark observing them with amused grins.

"I had a flat tire one time. I patched it with duct tape." Kellen shrugged. "It got me home."

Clark replied, "One time, I thought I broke my ankle. Duct taped it and walked around fine until I could get to the doctor."

Mischa waved her phone to point out the two men. "This, Faith, is why women live longer than men."

Kellen chuckled, "Which is why you will practice dancing with us."

"This should be fun." Mischa's eyes twinkled. "It's been a year since I've line danced. And the last time it was with my cousins."

"Please don't tell people the last part." Kellen pulled Mischa into a hug.

Faith heard the story one girl's night over wine. With her friends, Mischa presented a bubbly personality and was willing to try anything. Outside their small circle, Mischa was the definitive introvert who lingered close to family.

Last summer, one of Mischa's cousins married. It was an outdoor wedding at a nearby farm. The number of people overwhelmed Mischa. Her older cousin, Meryl, pulled her onto the dance floor to join the family.

According to Mischa, a good song was the only inspiration her family needed to dance. Spouses joined the line dance, and the wedding became the hootenanny the bride and groom intended.

Liam had a mixture of Paradise Hills and Hollywood friends in the ceremony. Holly had some of her friends as bridesmaids: Her sister Madison, Rebecca from the hair salon, Kim from the candy store, Faith, who fueled her taste for coffee, and Mischa, who was a doggy daycare owner. The other four bridesmaids were Liam's friends from Hollywood.

"I don't know why we need to practice." A blond who Faith would have sworn was a model from a shampoo commercial whispered to another bridesmaid who she thought she had seen in Liam's most recent movie. "Everyone knows how to do the Electric Slide."

Mischa mouthed the words to Faith, who shrugged her confusion. Faith murmured, "It sounds like a fire hazard to me.

"I thought we were doing the Achy Breaky Heart," Rebecca said to Kim.

"Isn't that the title of a television show from the nineties?" One of Liam's friends said.

The other replied, "No, it's a song by the father of Hannah Montana."

The snippets of conversation confirmed Liam and Holly's request to have a rehearsal. They needed to link the differences between Liam's past and future.

Liam hooked up his iPod to the sound system on the patio. He spoke through the microphone. "This first one will be easy. The song gives directions. Just listen." He clapped with the one-note beat that introduced the song. The tune was catchy,

Paradise Hills Summer

and Faith found herself torn between wanting to watch people before she joined the fun to just jumping in. The air around Kellen practically vibrated with energy. He positioned himself so he was on the right of Mischa. From there, people formed three rows of lines.

The next thing Faith knew, Toby Tucker, an up-and-coming country star, took her by the hand. "C'mon, let's have some fun." His smile encouraged her to clap along. It had been the first time a man other than Clark had given her attention in a fun setting.

Faith froze. She hoped the day would come when someone would see something in her that made her interesting. In her imaginings, she'd be confident and match the person step for step. The song told the dancers to go to the left. Instead of moving, Faith had to ask herself which direction was left.

Toby pointed, and she moved. "Just pay attention to me. You'll get it," he encouraged.

From that point on, the dance was fun. Faith was in sync with a large group of people.

It didn't matter that they came from different parts of the country.

Their relationship statuses didn't matter.

At that moment in time, Faith wasn't the woman who had to run away from home to find herself.

She was in sync with the world around her.

Laughter bubbled, illuminating the parts of Faith she had been hiding—even from herself. Faith took a good look at the person she had become, and she liked what she saw.

Then the music ended. People who had treated each other with indifference clapped and told strangers, "That was fun."

Toby tipped his chin down and quirked the corner of his lip into a sweet grin. "You're a quick learner."

The unease from earlier disappeared, and Faith returned the smile. "Thank you for helping me figure it out."

As quickly as the first song ended, the next song began. A banjo with a drum introduced a familiar Luke Bryan song. Three notes in, Faith recognized the music. The introduction of "Country Girls" by Luke Bryan was like receiving a phone call from an old friend. In a matter of seconds, Faith found Mischa and Kellen in the crowd. Their eyes connected, and the sense of anticipation heightened. This would be fun. The bridesmaids didn't say a word. They clapped in sync as they formed a line.

"Sorry, guys," Liam chuckled, "Holly asked me to play this song."

The men formed a line across from the women. When Luke Bryan's voice started the lyrics, the women stepped left and hooked their right foot behind them. Clark stood across from Faith. His steps mirrored Faith's.

Something about the atmosphere erased the pain caused by regret.

Faith and Clark were back in a time when life was simpler.

When he was the most important person in her world.

A spark in Clark's eyes reflected that he was in the same place.

The song ended, and everyone in the crowd clapped and hooted. Faith said to the bridesmaid, that looked like a shampoo model, "I thought you didn't know this dance."

The woman's face was flush with color from dancing. "If you know the steps to a few line dances, you know them all." Faith admired the confidence the woman used when she spoke. She took a better look at her. There was no doubting that the woman was drop-dead gorgeous. Her down-to-earth approach to the situation spoke more about why she was friends with Liam. The two women may come from two

Paradise Hills Summer

different worlds, but they had similar approaches to their problems.

Within two dances, the bridal party connected. It was no longer California vs. Montana. They became friends who came together to support and celebrate Holly and Liam's marriage.

It was what Faith wanted for her wedding. How Holly made it happen when Faith failed had her reassessing how she approached marriage. Was it the one thing that was out of her control or a compilation of actions that pushed Clark to end their relationship? The question blanketed the happiness of the prior moments.

"You're thinking too hard," Clark whispered.

The heat from Clark's breath tickled Faith's ear. She looked into his eyes and was brought back to their first date. Uncertainty and hope merged to create a tender expression. The objections warning Faith to be cautious around Clark's sexy ways fell silent. If he ever found out his superpower was those sincere, sweet glances, Faith would be a goner.

A slower-paced song came on. Clark held out his hand for Faith to accept. She set her hand in his. He wrapped his other hand around her back and pulled her toward him. His touch comforted her, and she tensed.

Faith didn't want to be comfortable with Clark. If she were comfortable, he could push her away again.

Like a moth to the flame, Faith walked into his trap. She set her hand on his shoulder and stepped closer. She wanted to sink into him and linger in the familiar feeling.

"I forgot how much fun we had when we danced." Clark pushed Faith away, twirled her, and pulled her back into him. Her body connected with and moved in tune with his.

When Clark tipped forward, Faith glided back.

When he took both her hands in his, she knew they would pretzel, untwist, and come back together.

With every complicated move, Faith fell in line and complimented Clark.

The dance sparked a memory. When life wasn't so complicated, Faith and Clark had so much fun together.

Her mother was right. If people had left Faith and Clark alone to solve their problems, she'd have a different last name.

Faith pushed aside the regret. There wasn't anything she could do to change the past. The best she could do was relish the present. The dance would end soon enough, and they'd separate. Faith wished the dance would never end.

The song ended with Faith and Clark standing in front of each other. Both, pleased with what they had done, grinned sweetly. Then something Faith never imagined happened. She wondered if they could do it again.

13

WRONG KIND OF PERFECT

Faith's eye caught Liam and Holly's mom wandering around the edges of tables with small trash bags in their hands. They picked up empty cups and dirty plates that people if given a chance, would have discarded.

Her conscience pricked her. When Faith was at the hotel, she overheard housekeepers mention how people got so caught up in their world, they forgot to pick up after themselves. Her eyes darted to where she had left her cup. Holly's mom was one table away from it. Faith hurried to the table and picked up her cup and two others beside it. "Sorry about that. I meant to put it in the trash." She set the cups in the bag.

"We're just trying to get ahead of the mess," Holly's mother replied. "It's easier to clean at ten p.m. than at eight a.m. Somehow the mess magnifies after a night of sleep."

Susan nudged her head to draw Stella's attention toward Holly and Liam. Liam had his hand on Holly's lower back. Both were listening to something Liam's older brother Hunter was saying.

Faith felt lucky to help with Liam and Holly's wedding. It softened the sting of all that had gone wrong in hers.

The sun rested on the horizon line, lighting the barbecue-turned-party. Until Holly's mother said anything, Faith hadn't realized so much time had passed. Earlier in the day, she promised herself that she'd hang out for a while and get home in time to watch a movie premiere on the Hallmark Channel.

"It looks like you're having fun," Holly's mother made her way to another table with a plate on the edge.

Faith followed behind her, intending to pick up a napkin that had blown into a bush. "I was. I mean. I am." She quickly corrected. She didn't want Holly and Liam's mothers to think helping them clean detracted from her enjoyment of the evening.

Liam's mother, Stella, pointed with her chin toward the men standing in a circle around the outdoor game at the edge of the lawn. "I would have laughed last summer if someone had told me I'd be hosting a barbecue for my youngest son's wedding party. But here we are."

"Liam and Holly are good for each other," Faith couldn't help grinning, especially when Holly told her the story of how she and Liam came together. Holly knew Liam was looking for someone but had no idea it was her. In a gesture of friendship, Holly tried setting up Liam with all her single friends.

"The way Toby looks at you has me thinking you two would make a cute couple," Susan gushed.

Faith felt warmth rise to her cheeks. It was sweet that other people thought she and Toby were cute together. Any woman would be a charming counterpart to the dark-haired, light-eyed, country singer.

Still, her heart leaned toward Clark...especially since he had changed his mind about her. The uncertainty that came with knowing Clark had the power to break her heart hampered

Paradise Hills Summer

Faith's ability to take the first step forward. An injured heart looked before leaping. It wasn't distrust in Clark. He'd never intentionally hurt her. Her heart learned the art of self-preservation.

Just then, Clark broke away from the game and scanned the yard. His eyes landed on Faith. He raised his brows and smiled. From across the yard, they could tell he was happy to see Faith.

Stella, who also witnessed the silent conversation, chuckled. "We called it wrong." She pushed a chair so it was closer to the table. "I'm glad I'm not single. I'd blow it."

Clark nudged the person next to him and said something. Faith's heart fluttered. She returned to the conversation. "It happens all the time at weddings. People see how happy the bride and groom are and form connections with someone they think is attractive."

"It happens when people least expect it," Stella cajoled. Holly also mentioned how Liam's parents, Stella and Marley, met under the town's famous tree. Stella spoke to Susan, "We should bring out some bowls of kettle corn." Both women left with their partially full bags toward the house, leaving Faith to stand alone at the edge of the party.

Faith took in the festivity happening all around her. Everyone seemed to get along. A group of the bridesmaids had gathered around a table by the door. Their shoes were on the ground beneath their chairs. Three of them used a chair to rest their feet while they reclined and talked. Their expressions conveyed the ease of speaking with someone whose companionship they enjoyed.

Mischa was at a table with Rebecca, Kim, and a friend they had met earlier in the evening. They had cards in their hand. Their heads bobbed with the music. Rebecca laid a card on the table, and the other three women threw their heads back in delighted disappointment.

"What are you smiling about?" Faith was so focused on appreciating the vibe she hadn't noticed Clark had come up alongside her.

"Tonight is perfect," Faith breathed in the floral summer air. She always loved the month of June when the lilacs were in full bloom.

"Ah, yes," he joined her appreciation, "You were always good at recognizing when things were perfect."

Faith didn't know how to interpret what he said. Was he reminiscing or reminding her why he broke up with her?

As soon as Faith heard about Clark's accident, she ran to the hospital. Faith didn't understand his decision to break off their engagement, but she was willing to let the hurt go. Clark needed her. Or so she thought. When she arrived at the hospital, he greeted her with a coldness that assimilated the Antarctic. "You're doing this so our friends will approve."

She attributed the ferocity as a side effect of the pain and let it slide. Clark broke a leg, his ribs were bruised, and his spine fractured. Faith was certain he would need her help while he recovered. "I was willing to be there for you in sickness and health." Faith, who was at the door, motioned to go further into the room. "I don't need to take your name to follow through with the promise."

"What I want is for you to give up the dream. It's over, Faith. We will never meet your ideal of perfect. Leave. Now." The cadence on the heart rate monitor increased.

Faith wanted to hurry to his bedside. Everything about the situation screamed that it would only make matters worse. So, she did what he asked. If she had known she would have been banned from the room, she would have stayed and tried to talk him down.

Paradise Hills Summer

It turned out Clark had the perfect plan to push her away.

Faith didn't want to be at the party anymore. The fun was too bright for her. It hurt her eyes to look into the sea of happy, beautiful people.

"Do you mind if I talk to you for a minute?" Heather, who Faith referred to as the shampoo model, twirled a strand of her hair.

Faith thought she would puke. The woman's overt flirtation with Clark disgusted her. Heather was gorgeous. There was no need for her to put herself on display for a man.

Clark's face brightened at the attention, and his posture straightened. "Sure. What's on your mind?"

Heather's eyes flicked toward Faith and back to Clark. "I wanted to make sure you could carve out a chunk of time for me." She rested her hand on Clark's forearm.

"I," Clark cleared his throat. "We can talk now." He shifted to face his back toward Faith.

Faith grumbled to herself. Thanks to Heather, she realized her pursuit of perfection wasn't superficial enough. When she and Clark were together, Faith tried to create the ideal home environment. With the new information, she realized Clark wanted a kind of perfect she hadn't been able to offer.

Annoyed by the shampoo model's beauty and Clark's reaction to it, Faith casually walked away from the conversation. Apparently, the conversation he started with Faith had come to a close.

14

RATHER INTENSE

Clark had enough problems. He didn't need Toby Tucker adding to them. His original plan was for Faith to see him in a natural environment. His mother taught him it took seven kind gestures to undo a mean word.

Clark had issued a long list of harsh words.

Selfish.

He called the woman who was willing to nurse him to health selfish.

That was after he broke up with her.

At the time, her sass angered him. She said, "I was willing to tell God and the world I'd love you through sickness and health. Just because we don't have a piece of paper doesn't mean my heart has changed."

He heard that she wanted what she wanted, and his feelings didn't matter.

Faith stepped out in faith of their enduring love.

Clark grinned at the irony of her name.

Well, turnabout was fair play. He had stuck his size twelve foot in his mouth and brought on the bad. Clark made a promise to himself to remind her of the good.

Paradise Hills Summer

Clark and Faith were in a natural setting. He had won the trust of her friends, so there would be no interruptions. His back hadn't been turned for less than a minute when Toby Tucker worked that country boy magic on Faith.

Even worse, Faith seemed to like it.

The woman flushed at something Toby said. And, the way she looked to him for direction when she was uncertain about the dance about undid Clark.

He wanted to go over there and set things right. But that's what got him in trouble in the first place. His temper. Clark let it go and hatched a new plan: find someone else to distract Toby.

Then Heather approached him. When she played with her long thick strands of hair, Clark sensed that she was on the prowl. She wasn't interested in him as much as she wanted a man to validate her beauty.

Heather was the 180-degree opposite of Faith, who was always making sure everyone else was happy.

The solution to Clark's problem walked up to him and said hello.

If Clark could get Toby together with Heather, he'd eliminate his problem and have Faith to himself.

Clark turned to tell Faith he'd be back in a minute to find she was halfway between him and the house. His shoulders tensed. Faith had never been this slippery when they lived with their family and friends. Then again, they always had someone to point them in the right direction.

In Paradise Hills, they were on their own. Worse, he had a row of tally marks against him. Clark was the man who parted by showing her the worst of him.

Heather's voice fought for his attention. "Do you want to go sit someplace quieter?"

Clark's eyes scanned the yard to find Toby. Toby was sitting on the edge of the fire pit with his guitar.

Then it clicked.

Women loved listening to the guitar by the fire.

"How about we go listen to Toby play."

Toby strummed a note on his guitar. When Clark tried to play the guitar, the instrument seemed to wail in protest at his touch. With one slide of his finger down the string, Toby had the thing humming like a dove calling out for its mate.

"Live music, in front of the fire, on a warm summer night." Heather's face softened. "I always thought the descriptions of country life were metaphors meant to make those of us who lived in the city jealous." She crooked her elbow with Clark's and motioned to go closer to the fire.

Clark straightened his elbow to release Heather's hold. "Let me go get us some seats."

Heather's quiet smile told him that one day, she would make some man happy. Clark hurried to retrieve two chairs from the tables. His eyes scanned the area for Faith. Where was she during all this?

He saw Holly and her sister with Liam's mother through the window.

A table of women worked together to clean up their game. One stuffed playing cards in a box while the others tapped them on the table and handed them to her.

Three others joined Heather at the fire. He set down two chairs. To the third woman, he said, I'll get you one.

"I got it." Liam's brother, Mark, set the two chairs he brought to add to the circle around Toby.

"I'll go get some drinks." Clark waited for Heather to tell him what she wanted.

Heather smiled appreciatively. "I'd like a lemonade."

It amazed Clark how quickly the situation changed. He

Paradise Hills Summer

wanted to talk to Faith. Catering to a beautiful woman was the furthest thing from his intentions, and Faith had disappeared entirely from the picture.

Clark nodded to Heather and went to the drink table. Mischa was there pouring herself a drink from the lemonade carafe. His time to get the information he needed was short. He asked Mischa, "Do you know where Faith went?"

Her brown eyes softened with apology. "She went home." Even though Mischa had accused Clark of being a stalker, he liked her. Faith had chosen a friend who spoke the truth. But one look in her eyes softened the harshness of reality. Despite what Mischa had said about Clark, she understood his intention. He was there to win the heart he had foolishly tossed away.

He replied with a hum of acknowledgment.

"I can imagine this is harder than she thought it would be. Especially with you here."

Mischa's statement was a punch below the gut. Clark didn't have to worry about anyone taking advantage of Faith. Her friends had taken up her cause and protected her. Mischa waited for him to finish filling the cup. "Did you plan on surprising her, or was it an honest coincidence?"

Liam and Clark went back a long way. Through mutual friends, they were in hunting parties together. When Liam learned about Clark's accident, he visited him in the hospital. This was toward the end of his hospital stay.

Clark didn't have time to complain about his breakup with Faith. Liam had just got engaged, and all he could talk about was Holly. When Clark wasn't sleeping, he worked out with Liam. Liam focused on getting stronger for a role in an upcoming movie, while Clark had to rebuild damaged muscles.

87

Everything changed, again, when Clark found the note. He went to Faith's family and apologized.

At first, they were angry, but lifelong family relationships won. Faith and Clark's fathers had been friends since school too. Their mothers had been friends almost as long.

Yes, he knew that Faith lived in Paradise Hills.

It was pure luck she had befriended Liam and Holly. "I'm not a stalker," he grumbled.

"I know," Mischa replied. "You're in love with her. Last question. I promise."

"Do I have a choice?" Clark crossed his arms in front of him and prepared himself for Mischa's inquisition.

"Good point," Mischa's right eye twinkled. "Why did you do it? Like, I mean, what happened? I've heard Faith's side of the story. I want to get yours."

Clark blew out a breath of air. He had been through a similar line of questioning with his mother. She cut him off so many times it took forever to get to the why. "When we were in school, the teachers always made us partners."

"Faith told me it was because you were smart, and she needed the help." Mischa's soft eyes conveyed her belief in what Faith had told her.

"She was being too nice," Clark loved how Faith could take a less-than-optimal situation and see how it benefited her. "I was an," he paused to choose the right word, "intense. I was an intense kid. Most people could only handle me in small chunks. But Faith. She could sit beside me all day."

At first, he was too young to realize he sat still when Faith was with him. Her presence calmed him. "One teacher talked to the next."

Every year it was Faith and Clark. "Except for the classes where they separated the boys from the girls, Faith and I were together for the entirety of our education. Anyway, I got this

Paradise Hills Summer

idea in my head that Faith was with me because she had to be. Not because she wanted to be. It was all I could think about. I thought a ceremony with just the two of us would be a clean start. It would prove to me that Faith married me because she wanted to, not because people set us up together." He shrugged. "Now, I know it was a stupid idea."

"It's funny how love changes us," Mischa mused. "Sometimes, it makes us stronger. Most of the time, it compels us to do some crazy things."

Clark and Mischa walked in silence and were inches out of earshot when she added, "Faith won't admit it, but she's still in love with you."

Clark stopped short.

How did Mischa know?

Had Faith said something?

Mischa tapped her temple with her pointer finger and answered the question Clark never got the chance to ask. "The same way I knew you were a stalker."

She sat in the chair beside Heather as though someone had intended it for her the whole time. "I have to ask. Do you use one type of shampoo or trade them out?"

Heather didn't seem to mind the change in plans. She glanced around as though she was getting ready to share trade secrets.

Clark never heard her answer. He didn't have to think twice when he saw the flick of Mischa's hand waving him away.

15

COLD FEET

Faith heard a deep sigh as her hand reached for the doorknob. She turned to find Holly hiding in the Lane's living room. "Is everything okay?"

Holly's tense jawline and shoulders pulled to her ears gave away the answer. Still, Holly replied, "Yes, I'm a little tired. Painting and all the people may have been a little too much." Holly was a hairdresser at the small salon on Main Street. Her capacity for conversation was within the small group spectrum. When she wasn't at the salon with three, maybe four people, Holly kept close to her friends and family.

"In a week, it will be down to two. You and Liam," Faith encouraged.

"Our courtship and engagement are fast. What if we're rushing and making the mistake of our lives?"

There was the problem. Holly had cold feet. "Do you see yourself with anyone other than Liam?"

Holly shook her head. "No."

"What would you be doing if you weren't with him right now?" Faith pried for more information. Perhaps Holly had an

Paradise Hills Summer

unfulfilled dream that would go unrecognized if they married. "Like, what would you be doing?"

Holly sat quietly. The answers flickered in her face as her eyes read through the reel in her mind. "I'd be at home watching cartoons with my nieces."

"Yes, marrying Liam would be a mistake," Faith joked. "Look at what he's pulling you away from. The Disney Channel and microwave popcorn."

Holly's shoulders lowered with the insight. "It isn't me I'm worried about." Her lips formed a thin line. "Clark called off your wedding a week before your ceremony. What if Liam changes his mind? He might think being with his friends is better than watching Netflix with me on the couch." Concern etched the corners of Holly's eyes.

Faith remembered Liam telling the story of the beginnings of his relationship with Holly. She turned to him for comfort in a dark movie theater. Holly thought a child was in danger, and she pressed herself into his chest as though being close to him would right the perceived forthcoming wrong. She trusted him. When Holly realized what she had done, she ran away. Liam spent days searching for the woman who gave him the one thing his friends couldn't provide. He felt needed. Liam fell in love with Holly because she wanted something fame didn't offer. She looked to him to chase away her fear of danger.

When Liam got too nostalgic, Holly would remind him with a playful chirp in her voice. He accused her of being a stalker. That got a laugh out of everyone.

"Clark is different than Liam." The confidence in Faith's voice struck her. "Once Liam had a vision of what he wanted." She pointed at Holly. "You. He chased after it until he got it. Remember the facial."

Holly chuckled. With the help of Holly's mother, Liam cornered Holly and proved he was in love with her.

This moment was her redemption. The awareness created a lightness in Faith's chest. Her pain relieved someone else's burden. She wished she hadn't lived getting dumped, but it was for the greater good.

"Thank you," Holly's face relaxed. She returned to the easygoing person who always suggested a hair trim and conditioning. "I hope one day to repay the kindness."

"You already have," Faith took Holly's hand in hers and gently squeezed it. "I should get going. I have an early date with a mare."

She rose, and Holly followed her to the door. Before Holly closed the door, she called out, "Stop by the salon. We got a new conditioner. I'll set aside some samples."

"Will do." Faith waved behind her and traversed the gravel road to her pickup. The sun had set, and a chill accompanied her view of the star-filled sky.

Faith briefly wondered if Holly mirrored Clark's reaction to matrimony. Clark lost it a week before their wedding. She only had his letter to provide insight.

In the short proposal to elope, Clark mentioned concerns about their friends' influence and wanting some time when it was only the two of them. Then again, his interest in the shampoo model had Faith questioning his motive.

What if pressure from their friends prompted his proposal? Everyone expected Clark and Faith to get married. They dated through high school and college. The hints came when they didn't follow the natural progression. Faith loved Clark enough to wait for him. Since they graduated from college, he had been on the rodeo circuit, tried selling insurance, and settled into a job as the maintenance engineer for their small town. The man could fix anything.

Paradise Hills Summer

If she learned anything this past year, it was that only she was responsible for mending her own broken heart.

16

THE FALL

It had been a while since Faith needed to have a chat with Skye. The human-horse connection amazed her. Once, she asked Willy how the horse discerned her emotions. He replied, "It's a gift older than time."

Faith guessed that was his way of saying he didn't know and was okay with it. Some things didn't need an explanation. It was best to accept the blessing with gratitude and repay it when the time was right.

Faith's shoulders lightened, and her lungs found the space to expand with the faint scents of hay and freshly kicked-up soil. She meandered into the stable, taking in the muted colors the soft morning light created. Skye bobbed her head in greeting.

"I told you I'd return this weekend." To some people, Skye was just a horse. To Faith, Skye was the companion that kept her centered when her world had been turned upside down. Now she was back for reinforcement.

After her conversation with Holly, like blocks within a moving structure, all the pieces that made Faith's character

Paradise Hills Summer

shifted to form a new identity. This one seemed sturdier. She didn't need validation from Clark.

Something within her tightened the core of her being. She loved herself. Her hair wasn't perfect. She chuckled. For some reason, Clark's attraction to the hair model bothered her more than it should have. Faith shifted her focus on what mattered. Her heart had shown itself. Faith was the type of person who made people feel better about themselves. It was a character trait the world needed.

Faith committed to expanding the skill. When she handed the cup of coffee over the counter, she'd offer an encouragement, a smile, a thank you for being you, a statement recognizing the person's essence. She held out a handful of sliced apples. Skye wriggled her lips to take in the chunks. "Thank you,"

Skye paused briefly. She shook her head and returned to enjoying the surprise Faith brought her.

When the cinnamon-colored horse finished the snack, she backed away. Their conversation was over. Faith pivoted to leave and saw movement in the corner of her peripheral vision.

"What was that?" Faith exclaimed. The animal meandered into the light. What Faith hoped was a kitten was, in fact, a baby skunk. Taking a note from the horse's book, Faith reversed her motion. She backed into something that created a chain of events she could not duplicate if she tried. She bumped into a rake that hit a bucket. It dropped with a clang that sent the skunk skittering toward her. Without regard to where she was headed, Faith bolted into a half-open stall. She clotheslined herself and fell to the ground. Skye's horsey chuckle set the tone for her last remembrance of what happened before the mist filled the entrance to the barn.

Skye neighed in disgust as if she were saying, "Look at the mess you made." The horse rotated in a circle within the stall. As hard as it tried, there wasn't any place to avoid the scent that wafted in their direction. Faith's eyes watered, and a gag reflex had her gut wrenching.

If that wasn't bad enough, Willy's voice came through the barn doors. "What in green acres do they got going on in there!"

There was a momentary pause for what she guessed was the other person's voice.

"It's coming this way!"

Faith watched the skunk waddle out of the barn. While the skunk hadn't sprayed her directly, she suspected the scent had attached to her clothes. Skye bobbed, swung her head, and whinnied. The horse was just as uncomfortable as Faith with the situation.

The sun behind Willy gave him a shadow effect. Faith caught the outline of his body passing through the doorway before she bent over and gagged. She covered her mouth and nose with her hand to filter out the smell. Faith's first attempt to run from disaster didn't work. Surely, a second attempt would yield success.

In her mind, she would dash through the door, and the clean air would refresh her senses. She prayed the skunk spray hadn't burned the lining of her nose.

Willie turned to the person who accompanied him. "I get the feeling you're going to have to change your plans for the afternoon."

If Faith had the power to inhale, she would have gasped. The other person was none other than Clark. Faith bet he brought the shampoo model there for a ride. She groaned inside. She should have kept her plan for the afternoon a secret.

Paradise Hills Summer

Bitterness turned her stomach sour. As she sided her way around Clark and Willie, Faith spoke through her hand. "I'm sorry, Willie." She trusted Willie to free Skye from the stall and maintained her course to a place as far away as possible from the skunk scent.

"Are you okay, Faith?" Clark caught up to Faith and walked alongside her.

It didn't make sense to Faith that Clark was following her. First, she smelled like death. Second, she presumed he was there to entertain Heather. Faith didn't want to ruin their afternoon too. "Yes, I'll be fine after I have a peroxide and dish soap shower." Her skin itched, thinking about how dried it would be after she used the dishwashing liquid combination as a body wash. If Holly thought Faith needed conditioner before, she was in for a surprise.

Clark grimaced. "I can give you a ride home."

"Aren't you here with a date?" Faith would never have taken Clark to be a player. But what else could she conclude? He came to the stables to ride horses with one woman and offered to leave with another.

Clark held his hands out in front of him. "Who would that be." He turned his attention to the area around them, emphasizing his point.

Off in the open area, a family with two young school-aged children was talking to a pony. A hostler that looked close to Clark's age carried a bucket with grooming supplies toward the barn. He stopped short when his nose picked up the skunk scent. There were other people and other animals, and none of them resembled the woman who made Faith feel like a failure.

She altered the course of the conversation. "I thought you were helping Liam entertain his out-of-town guest." Given the circumstances, it was the best she could come up with. Faith was not about to admit that she was jealous.

MERRI MAYWETHER

Clark pinched the sides of the scruff on his chin to hide the grin that had formed at the corner of his mouth. "No, I heard this was a good place to visit to get away from it all. I thought I'd check it out."

A horse's neigh in the distance grabbed both of their attention. It sounded like Skye was telling Willie what Faith had done to cause the minor disaster in the barn.

Faith's head hurt thinking about what they needed to do to eliminate the smell. The least she could do was offer to help clean the horse. "Excuse me. I need to talk to Willie."

She pivoted on her foot and headed toward the barn. Skye snorted her disgust and faced away. Undeterred by the horse's justifiable attitude, Faith approached Willie, who opened the gate to the corral. The chestnut mare walked into and trotted to the middle of the coral.

"I'm sorry about what happened in the barn. As soon as I get cleaned up, I can come out and help with the mess." Faith's nose burned. She wondered if there was a way to clean her sinuses.

"Don't worry about it. We have gallons of odor eliminator. I'll have Brad hit the barn with a power washer, and we'll put some fresh hay in there. It won't get rid of the smell, but it'll be bearable."

"I can help with the hay." Faith missed being on the farm. Hitting the hay with a pitchfork would be cathartic, and she'd feel like she had helped with the solution to the problem. If she hadn't bumped into the shovel, the bucket dropping wouldn't have scared the skunk.

Willie leaned away from Faith. "How about you take care of yourself, and then we can talk."

"C'mon, let's get you cleaned up." Clark tugged at Faith's elbow. He tipped his head toward Willie. "Thanks for helping me find her."

Paradise Hills Summer

Mocking like he was plugging his nose, Willie replied. "She did that on her own."

17

LIKE OLD TIMES

Good intentions could motivate a person so far before they questioned the logic of their decision. On those grounds, Faith refused to ride home with Clark. As it was, she rode in her own pickup with all the windows open.

Whenever Faith had the chance, she poked her head out the window for fresh air. By the time she pulled into the driveway of her small cottage-style house, she'd decided her once favorite jeans were destined to end up in the trash bin.

The first thing she did when she walked in the front door of her house was strip down to her undergarments. The less she trailed into the house, the less she'd have to clean afterward.

Free of the garments that held most of the residue of the mist, Faith started to feel better. She collected the ingredients she needed: baking soda, dish soap, peroxide, and a washcloth and set them on her counter. The foaming mixture looked more like a science experiment that could go wrong than a concoction that would free her of the awful odor misfortune had delivered.

Faith applied the mixture to her arms and legs. It foamed but didn't burn as she feared. The more she used, the better

Paradise Hills Summer

she felt. She imagined the bubbling substance eating away at the invisible molecules that made her head hurt and her skin crawl. Careful to keep any of it from dripping into her eyes, Faith used the washcloth to coat her hair in the miracle substance. As she massaged it into her scalp, the feelings of normalcy returned. She was a rinse away from being Sunday Faith. The version of herself that walked around the house in yoga pants and an oversized t-shirt.

The tinny scent of warm water confirmed Faith's cleanliness. Her sinuses were still sensitive, but her fears of the skunk scent lingering trailed down the drain.

"Make sure you rinse it good," Willie cautioned. He added, "And make sure to pour what you have left down the pipes and flush them with water."

With one towel wrapped around her chest and the other resting on her head like a lavender turban, Faith followed the instructions as best as she could remember. A knock on her door pulled at her attention. Because Faith hadn't expected any guests, she couldn't guess who was at the door.

Faith hustled to get into a robe and called out, "I'll be there in a minute!"

Out of breath, Faith peeked through a crack in the door. Clark held out a small pink gift bag. He was wearing a navy short sleeve v-neck shirt and longer camouflage shorts. Sunglasses and his Montana Grizzly baseball cap shielded his face. "I stopped by the spa at the hotel. The ladies there said this might help you feel better."

Faith grasped the front of her robe with one hand to secure it to her chest. She opened the door wider with the other hand. "You didn't have to do that. Willie's de-skunking recipe worked wonders. I feel like a new person."

Clark's jaw tightened to show his disappointment.

Faith wished she could grab at the words and take them

back. Clark was trying to do something kind for her, and she hadn't acknowledged it. "I'm sure whatever you brought will make me feel like a queen."

Clark shuffled in place. Faith noticed his fingers fiddling with the bag handle as he handed it to her.

"Let me change into something more appropriate, and I'll open it." Faith stepped away from the door to invite him into the room.

Clark positioned his glasses on the back of his hat to give her a clear view of his brown eyes. He took in a breath, and his smile softened. "I can do that."

Faith realized how much she missed the smile. Growing up with Clark allowed her to see the many variations of his smiles. The one he gave when he felt appreciated was his most attractive. It starkly contrasted the snarl that ran her out of Castle Hill. The recollection of the other side of Clark cooled the warmth of the remembrance.

The conflict between hurrying and trying not to look like she was rushing tore at Faith. She tried telling herself that it was just Clark. They had known each other forever. It wasn't like Faith had to impress Clark. Still, something in her wanted him to like her.

Faith stopped in front of her closet. She took a breath and murmured to herself. "Everybody wants to be liked." The desire to impress wasn't because she had feelings for Clark. It was the basic need of appreciation all people have. In her talks with Skye, Faith declared that one person's opinion mattered. Her own. It amazed her at how quickly she backslid.

Clark sat straight against the back of the couch. He rubbed his palms on the leg of his pants. "I had fun yesterday."

Faith drew up the image of Clark with the hair model. She bet he had fun. However, it was contrary to her nature to point it out when Clark did things that bothered her. It was a piece

Paradise Hills Summer

of advice Faith's mother ingrained in her when she was a small girl. Men don't need us sharing what's wrong with them. They get plenty of that from the world. It's our job to tell them what they're doing right. Faith faked a smile and pushed forward with the conversation. "Did you know they were having a dance rehearsal?"

"No, but I could have suspected as much." A glimmer of Clark's sarcastic grin appeared. He smiled with half his mouth while the other half remained straight. "Liam rehearses everything. Before he works out, he talks through his routine. It's like he has a director with him at all times."

When Holly talked about Liam, she shared the sweet things he did around her. He loved reading through magazines and commenting on the styles. At the time, Faith thought Holly should be concerned. Then Holly explained that Liam knew a lot of makeup artists. He made sure he had something kind or thoughtful to say to them when they worked together on the set. Faith marveled at the difference in perspective. Clark saw a planner, while Holly saw a man who looked for ways to make people comfortable.

The more time Faith spent with Clark, the more she realized it was better that they hadn't married. She was a different person since she left Castle Hill, Montana. During her time away from the influences of her childhood, a personality she never expected emerged. Faith still enjoyed doing things to make people happy, but she didn't do it at the expense of her joy. When people asked Faith what she wanted to do, she told them without the constant concern of disappointing them.

She relaxed, knowing that things turned out like they were supposed to. At the time when things went awry, it hurt her heart. Hindsight proved that Clark and Faith saved themselves from a string of unpleasant experiences.

"It was like old times." Clark's eyes darted to the pictures of Faith's family. Instead of losing the deposit to the photographer, they had a family photoshoot. Faith's brother unmercifully antagonized her. Her father pointed out that although they were grown, Faith and Matthew still argued like an older sister and younger brother. The comment elicited warm grins of appreciation toward each other. *It was like old times.* Matthew wrapped his arm around Faith's neck and pulled her into a hug. The photographer snapped the picture. Her father and mother were on the side with smiles that expressed pride in their children. The photo reminded Faith that life's most precious moments came when things didn't turn out the way people planned.

"I miss hanging out with your family on the weekends."

Faith arched her eyebrow. "That's not the way I heard it."

"What's that supposed to mean?" The falter in Clark's voice betrayed his denial.

"Matthew told me you two have a weekly meeting via Xbox." Faith raised a finger to cut off Clark's objection. "And our parents play cards every Thursday night."

"But it isn't with you." Clark leaned forward and clasped his hand before setting them on his knees. "I miss getting annoyed when you want our outfits to match. I miss eating half your fries because you always order too many. Most importantly, I miss how you could convince me that the only thing that mattered was how we felt about each other."

Faith couldn't believe he got all that from one dance. She was keenly aware that she didn't have to think about the direction they moved or worry if they were in sync with the tempo. The familiarity with the way Clark moved calmed her. But not enough to draw her to the conclusion that life with him was better than life without him. She didn't have a reply for him.

"Don't you miss us?"

Paradise Hills Summer

"I used to," Faith admitted. "But then I learned how to like living by myself."

Clark jerked back at her response. "How is that possible? You're an amazing person."

"Because I was doing what you wanted." Faith couldn't look Clark in the eye. "I left Castle Hill because you didn't want to see me again. I'm staying in Paradise Hills because I like it here."

Clark's face twisted like someone had punched him in the gut. "I didn't mean it."

"Did you decide before or after you found the missing note?"

His silence answered her question.

She didn't want to be right. Faith wanted to be happy. It would be easier to fall into the role of morphing into the person people expected her to be. Happiness meant being true to the person she had to talk to when nobody was there. Faith was about to say that Clark didn't love her. He loved the memories.

Instead, he threw her for a loop when he said, "I feel bad for saying this. I like the new you better."

18

PROVED ME RIGHT

Clark's last conversation with Mark Alexander echoed somewhere in the back of his mind.

Faith's father squeezed Clark's shoulder. "If you hurt my daughter again, I will hurt you." The lines in her father's weather-worn face emphasized the stern look in his eyes.

"I'll be too busy making it up for the rest of my life to worry about that," Clark admitted. He had never made such a big mess of things.

Faith's reaction in the restaurant. Clark expected it. He caught her unaware. The Faith he remembered from Castle Hill would avoid him. She liked to make people happy. When she couldn't do it, she ran.

The woman in front of him. She had hints of Faith from the past. This one had his mind spinning in all directions. She wasn't seeing anyone else, so her independence wasn't loyalty to another man.

Faith was beyond beautiful in those sweats that hung low on her hips and a loose t-shirt. This Faith cared more about being comfortable. Clark wanted her to nuzzle up with him on

Paradise Hills Summer

the couch and watch a movie. Then he'd be able to smell the lotion he bought her from the spa.

When Clark said, "I like you better this way," Faith's mouth opened slightly. Why it shocked her, made no sense to him. She liked her new life. Clark loved her can-do spirit. Not that he didn't enjoy helping Faith in the past, but admiration swelled in him when Faith insisted that she could take care of the skunk spraying on her own.

Clark cleared his throat, and his palms were getting sweaty. He rubbed his hands on the front of his shorts. "By the way, you proved me right."

"What do you mean?" Her voice rose in agitation. The glints of blond in her hair seemed to sparkle. They added a softness to her face.

Remembering what went wrong brought a tint of sadness to his voice. "I worried that the wedding was about making our friends happy."

Faith pursed her lips at his assessment.

Clark continued, "That you were getting married because it was something people expected us to do." Faith said the right things at the right time. But he noticed as the date to the wedding approached, the slightly defiant glint in her eye dimmed. When she looked at him, it was as though he wasn't there, and Faith was reading through a list of things she needed to do that day. "I wanted to start our marriage with a statement that it was you and me… us against the problems."

"But, our friends were there to support us." She waved her hand like they were in the room. "They were the ones who we called when we had a project bigger than us. Or if I had a problem and didn't know the answer, I called them. The wedding was their way of saying they'd be there for us and our way of saying we'd turn to them."

"You are correct," Clark said. "And you wanted them to be

happy. Everything had to be.... I believe you said the word was perfect."

"I was speaking metaphorically. Everybody knows something can go wrong at a wedding."

"Yes, and you like the way things are now because you don't have to care about what people think. Isn't that close to saying you don't have to be perfect?"

Faith didn't quite gasp, but a soft noise escaped her lips before she clamped her mouth shut. She inhaled a breath. "I loved you."

Clark searched Faith's face to connect with her. She was present, but there was a thin veil keeping her at the edge of the conversation.

"You still do." Clark clasped his hands together. "I see it in the way you avoid looking me in the eye. You're at the corner of the conversation peeking in. You do that when you're hiding something."

One time when they were dating, Faith borrowed his pickup. Someone crashed their cart into it. She had a couple of friends with her to help her explain. Faith started with, "I have something to tell you that will make you mad." She tilted her chin toward her body. The top of her eyes was focused someplace else. The expression was so guilt-ridden Clark feared she had rolled the pickup. "I had a situation with your pickup." The first thing that mattered was her safety. "Are you okay?" He searched for any visible signs of injury.

"Yes, I'm fine," Faith grimaced and added, "but there is a scratch the size of my hand near the rear tire."

Talk about specific details. Clark chuckled every time he thought back on the moment. Her friends took over, explaining how they were in the store, and found the cart leaned against his wheel well.

Clark didn't care about the pickup or her friend's explana-

Paradise Hills Summer

tions. It bothered him that Faith thought he valued the pickup more than her well-being. If Faith's friends weren't there, Clark would have taken her hands into his, looked her in the eye, and said, "Darling, we will have dents. You are more important to me than a pickup we'll probably replace in three or four years." Because her friends were there, he had to contend with them. So, Clark said, "It's nothing a couple of beers and a couple of hours in the garage won't fix."

He must have said the right thing because she came out of hiding. She looked him in the eye, and the sparkle was there. "You're not mad?"

He said something flirty, and all three women giggled. He overheard one of the other two women say, "My dad would have come loose if I dented his pickup." When the wary looks surfaced closer to the wedding date, Clark wasn't sure if it was cold feet or her friends filling Faith with ideas of what life would be like once they married.

As quickly as his mind flashed to the past, it was back in Faith's living room.

"I have no reason to hide," Faith sassed. To make her point, she adjusted her gaze. Her eyes connected with his, and he saw what he had been looking for. The fire from when they were younger. When he challenged her, and she thought she could beat him. It was the fire that made him slow down so she could catch up to him.

"Exactly," Clark held out his hands like she had just arrived at the same conclusion as him. "We should be able to look each other in the eye and tell each other the truth. We still love each other."

A slight smirk formed on her lips, but then it softened. "Look, Clark, what we had was special." Her pause gave away the struggle Faith was having with the conversation.

Clark saw it in her eyes. The look confirmed what he had

worried about six months ago. It had been a long time since Faith had been truthful with Clark. "I will always love you, but it is time to move on."

Moving on and moving forward were the same thing. Clark wanted to say as much, but he had a plan. Faith had to think she won. Clark nodded to let her know he understood. He looked her straight in the eye and said, "You are beautiful when you're stubborn," and shook his head like she was a puzzle he couldn't quite piece together. He rose, "You've heard what I came to say."

The disappointment on her face was more informative than the entire set of World Book Encyclopedias. She wanted him to fight for her. He said, "Thank you for hearing me out," and headed for the door.

19

STILL IN LOVE

*F*aith hardly slept.
Clark!
The man aggravated her.

He visited her house under the guise of bringing her a present. Then he told her, not asked her, she was still in love with him, called her beautiful, and left her there alone with her thoughts.

He hadn't been gone an hour when he texted her. "This is Clark. I have a question."

She intended to ignore the text. Within a few minutes, he texted again. "I can see the dots when you read my texts."

It was like they were in high school again. Whenever Clark wanted attention, he badgered her. It was cute, then. But now they were adults, and she had things to do. She eyed the dirty laundry, returned to the text, and quickly typed, "What?"

"Bacon or Sausage?"

Faith groaned. He was playing this or that?

Whenever there was a lull in a conversation, he'd pull out this or that. The questions could be simple or complex. He'd point to a landmark. In a race, who do you think would make it first? Sometimes it was an animal; others, he'd present the question with professional athletes. It worked every time.

"I'm not playing," Faith replied.

"How can I surprise you with breakfast if I don't know?"

This time her response came quickly, "Just don't get me breakfast."

Hook, line, and sinker. Faith fell into a text conversation with Clark that lasted two hours. It was long enough for her not to notice that her hair had gone from dark brown to some auburn color until it was too late to go to a salon. So, she texted Holly. She learned hairstylist rule number one: skunk soap made with hydrogen peroxide is not for hair... especially color-treated hair.

To hide that she had gone from a brunette to a redhead, she tied her hair into a bun and used a thick headband to hide the rest of it. She crawled into work a little before six in the morning with a cloud over her head.

Once Faith was at the coffee kiosk, her perspective changed. She had plenty to distract her from Clark. Misty had already brewed the coffee and set the creamers out on the customer side of the counter.

Then the yellow flags dropped.

Something was awry.

Misty was early.

Early enough to have the coffee finished before Faith arrived at the kiosk.

Misty spent most of her free time online playing video games and was usually five to ten minutes late.

"Good morning," Faith pushed her smile forward. "You're here early."

"Hm mm." Misty ducked down to retrieve the lids from the bottom cabinet. She rose and refreshed the dispenser.

She was either distracted or mad. Faith replayed the last

Paradise Hills Summer

time they talked. Everything seemed fine. "Did something happen?"

"What would happen?" Misty's voice rose just the same way women said nothing when something was, in fact, bothering them.

Had Faith promised to do something and failed to come through? Did she say something that could have been interpreted differently after the fact? Had Misty heard about the skunk situation and thought Faith was responsible? With each question, the answer was no. What could have happened between Friday and Monday? "You seem a little tense," Faith replied.

"Maybe I'm tense because someone I know was engaged to the human Hercules and never mentioned it."

The anger in Misty's voice went straight to Faith's heart and gripped it. Without intending to, Faith had hurt Misty's feelings. "I. Ah." The words wouldn't come to her, so she took a breath. "Because."

Misty held her arms in front of her chest and scowled while waiting for the explanation.

"I was trying to forget." Faith exhaled a breath. "I thought by moving here, I'd be able to go on with life and forget the past ever happened. It turns out life has a way of reminding us of our mistakes. I guess that's where humility comes from."

The frown on Misty's lip quivered. She fought for a second and then cracked. A small smile took over her expression. "Smart people learn from their mistakes. How being engaged to a man that looks like he could open a can with his bare hands was a mistake is beyond me."

"It's complicated," Faith explained. Since she and Clark had been together for their entire lives, Faith had taken Clark's attractiveness for granted. She knew him when he was a husky boy who always had seconds.

113

He gradually changed when they were in high school. His height caught up with his weight, and his participation in sports added to the bulk. Because Faith was there for the small, day-to-day changes, she had taken for granted the person Clark had become.

Faith compared how she regarded Clark with how the hair model talked to him. Her heart pinched. She always treated Clark like he was that nine-year-old boy that rode his bike ahead of her. Yes, their situation was complicated.

Misty turned to one of the upper cabinets and pulled out the container that held the sugar packets. "Well, if you hear his side of the story, he hasn't forgotten."

Faith didn't want to hear it. Yet she did. All people had the desire to be wanted. But was it right for her to enjoy it from Clark? She told him that things were over with him. The fair thing to do was to push aside the feelings and hope that he forgot.

His rich voice slid into their conversation. "Good morning."

Faith, who had her back to the counter, made eye contact with Misty. They asked how long Clark had been standing there. Misty, equally absorbed in the discussion, shrugged to say she didn't know.

When Faith turned around, she gave him her coffee kiosk smile. "Good morning. Were your ears burning?" She might as well confront the situation. If he heard them talking about him, she could explain.

"No, why?" Clark's eyes darted from Faith to Misty and back to Faith as though he were trying to read the situation.

Ha, she had the upper hand for once. "You were with me for how long and did not mention that my hair was a different color than the day before?"

Clark leaned away to avoid the waves of anger coming off

Paradise Hills Summer

Faith. "I noticed something different." He made a circular motion to point in her general direction. "But I thought it was because you weren't made up. Women look different when they're comfortable versus when they're trying to impress someone."

"He has a point there," Misty sided with Clark. To Faith's dirty look, she whimpered, "At least I do."

Then Clark winked his thanks to Misty. Faith stiffened as the lightning bolt of jealousy coursed through her. She inhaled. "What can we get for you?"

"I'll just have a coffee." Clark flashed her a grin.

With the added perspective from Misty's insight, Faith noticed Clark was a mixture of sweet and sexy. Her heart skipped a beat and then lurched. She was trying to forget that she cared about Clark, not deepen her admiration for him. "Here you go," she set the small cup in front of him, and he laid his dollar on the counter. Before she got caught deeper into his snare, she excused herself.

He followed her to the other side of the kiosk. "What time do you have lunch today?"

"I don't eat lunch." Technically, she hadn't lied. She nibbled on her lunch throughout the day. That gave her time to visit the stables and spend time with Skye.

"Too bad," Clark shrugged, took his coffee, and disappeared down the corridor to the gym.

After knowing Clark for her entire life, Faith should have known it would not be as easy as passing Clark a cup of coffee and going on with her business. Her eyes followed him. There was something about the way he casually strolled that had her catching her breath.

Misty said, "I love it when a man who can wear athletic wear actually does it."

As if he heard her, Clark turned toward the kiosk and

caught both women gawking at him like he was a plate of chocolate in the middle of a salad bar. He grinned, raised his cup like he was toasting the women, and returned to the entrance to the gym.

"Busted at six in the morning."

Faith burst into a fit of giggles at Misty's exclamation.

20

LOOK FOR THE SIGN

When Faith sent a text message with the picture of her hair, Mischa and Holly ran into action. They made calls and set aside time for damage control. Rebecca, the salon owner, worked on Faith's hair while the others discussed what they needed to do in the next few days. They all hoped that by the end of the styling session, Faith would look less like a cartoon character and more like a real person.

Holly, Mischa, and Heather ended up offering moral support. They sat in a circle around Holly and Rebecca. "Let me get this straight." Mischa raised a finger with each question. "Clark came to your house? After you were skunked? With scented lotion from the spa?"

"Yes."

Mischa's investigative reporter tone set Faith on edge. What obvious sign had she seen that eluded Faith?

Holly's brows furrowed. "Did you make a wish?"

"Does asking him to disappear count?"

Holly and Mischa held a silent conversation. Their eyes

flashed, and one shook her head to negate whatever the other said.

Faith and Heather exchanged glances and had a nonverbal discussion of their own. Neither knew what the other two had said, and they didn't like the left-out feeling.

Faith found it ironic that when she was at her worst, she became allies with the woman she despised two days prior. On Saturday, she'd only allowed herself to acknowledge Heather by her attention-garnering beautiful hair.

Holly's hands were on Heather's arms when she ushered her to a position in front of Faith. "You tell her, she'll never believe me." Heather groaned, and Holly added, "I can't get her to condition correctly. What makes you think she'll buy into hair extensions."

"Hair extensions?" Faith analyzed Heather's hair. The color progressed, starting with the roots being a shade lighter than the ends. The ends rolled into the fat barrel curls.

Faith had witnessed the magic of the barrel curl. Clark practically melted when Heather twisted them around her finger.

The highlights added a shine that tempted people to touch it. Faith searched but didn't find signs of glues or bumps from the elastic or combs used to attach the hair.

"If you saw how often my hair gets styled in one photo shoot." Heather pulled on a strip of hair. "Normal hair cannot withstand the abuse. It cracks and breaks."

"But you're a hair model, isn't that false advertising?"

"I'm not a hair model." Heather seemed taken aback by Faith's assumption. "I'm a swimsuit model."

Faith groaned. Not that she cared, but there was no way Clark, or any other man, would find any interest in her when she was standing beside a swimsuit model.

Paradise Hills Summer

"Focus," Mischa snapped her fingers in front of Faith's face.

"What were we talking about?" The mist cleared away from Faith's mind, and she was back in the conversation.

"Signs. We're looking for signs."

"Signs of what?" Faith kept her head stiff to avoid interfering with Rebecca's repair job.

"A sign that proves you are destined to be together," Rebecca replied.

Holly gave the first example. "Well, Liam made a wish beneath the old tree. Then I left a pin in the theater. He took it as a sign."

"And Kellen's grandmother waved her shamrock wand over me at Bingo when Kellen and I met." Mischa grinned. "We've been together ever since."

Rebecca tapped Faith's shoulder. "Paradise Hills believes in the magic of love. Not that love is magic. Love is concrete and takes a lot of effort to sustain. It just shows itself in ways that seem magical."

"What happened to the old way of having butterflies in the stomach and not being able to sleep or eat because you're always thinking about the other person," Faith asked.

"I like cookies too much," Holly answered.

"You've been here long enough to know the food is too good to waste on angst," Mischa added. "Speaking of. I hear there's huckleberry pie across the way."

All the women's eyes trailed out the window like they would see the cafe two doors away from the hair salon. Clark, Liam, and Kellen passed by the front of the salon in the cafe's direction.

"If I know Liam, he'll bring me some pie," Holly beamed.

Faith's eyes burned, and she blinked away a tear. Holly's confidence in Liam's affection for her touched her heart. And therein lay the problem. Sign or no sign, Faith would never trust a man's love again.

Without warning, Clark turned on her. She never saw it coming. If Faith had an inkling that he was in a place where he could change his mind so quickly, she wouldn't have been so surprised by the outcome.

But the entire time, she listened to her heart of hearts. It painted a picture of them together in old age. Even though they weren't a couple, Faith still had the mental image of them gray-haired, walking along holding hands. Her head, wisened by experience, refused to allow her heart to trust Clark or any man ever again.

"We had our sign." The answer came to Faith so quickly that it gave her a sudden headache.

"What was it?" The women tilted closer into the conversation.

"The note. The note that never made it to me. It was a sign of the disconnect." Faith wanted to cry. Secretly she hoped she was wrong. But according to the law of signs, she and Clark weren't meant to be together.

"That's not a sign," Mischa balked. "You have to be in Paradise Hills for it to be a sign."

"Who made that rule?" Faith's disappointment made her sound crankier than she intended. "I'm sorry. I meant to say." She searched for words, but nothing better came to mind. "Who sets limitations on signs?"

"Does your town believe in signs?"

Faith chuckled at the irony. Her father managed a small store. They had signs all over the place. "We have too many to know which ones are important."

"There you go," Mischa rubbed her hands together like the matter had been resolved. "We just need to keep an eye out for the sign."

Paradise Hills Summer

The sound of the door opening behind them drew their attention to the front of the hair salon. Liam, Kellen, Clark, and Toby appeared with bags in their hands. "We come bearing gifts."

The door slammed into Toby, who pushed Clark to the side.

Clark threw him an annoyed frown.

Toby gestured behind himself with his thumb. "The door. You guys didn't make enough room."

Toby stopped, and his eyes seemed to read a scrolling of words visible only to him. He murmured, "That would be a good theme for a song." He whipped out his phone and tapped at the keys.

Liam beamed, "We can all say we were here when he found his inspiration for a song."

Kellen joked, "I hope it isn't don't let the door hit you on the backside."

Mischa's guffaws sent off a chain of laughter. Amid the delight, Clark's eyes connected with Faith's. Something Faith's father used to say when she was younger came to mind. "Love holds no records of wrong."

With the subtle message, a wave washed over Faith. Like the skunk soap, it removed the harshness of the foul spray of mistrust and gave her doubt a different hue.

21

BEST SUMMER EVER

Love forged bonds. Burned by the fire, Faith maintained a healthy distance. While she didn't trust Clark's resilience, she admired him for having it.

One by one, her friends not only accepted but seemed to embrace Clark's friendship as well as his intention. His actions proved him worthy in their eyes.

Faith found herself asking the question, what would it take to get her to forget the hurt? She wanted to like Clark the way her friends did.

Kellen and Mischa were the first to leave the salon. Holly and Liam followed, dwindling the group to five. Heather and Toby compared mutual friends. It turned out they ran in the same circles and had never met. They carried the conversation over to Heather's Airbnb.

The evening wasn't that much different than if they were at home. Clark or Faith would wind up at the other's house and work on a project together. Sometimes it was just dinner and cleaning up afterward. Because of Faith's fiasco, Rebecca had to work late. Faith offered to help with the cleanup. When

Paradise Hills Summer

Rebecca balked, Faith said, "I'd feel better if you let me throw some towels in the washer."

Clark dusted and chatted with Rebecca, who damp-mopped the floors. Rebecca, who seemed to enjoy the company, told Faith and Clark about the sources of the decorations around the salon. The shelf that held framed pictures of friends came from a local artist. The styling knickknacks were gifts from two of her older models.

Rebecca spoke of her clientele like they were friends or close family. When they finished cleaning, she turned off the lights and locked the door behind them. She walked with Clark and Faith up to the café. Rebecca stopped to visit the owner, and Faith continued to go home.

Paradise Hills was just as beautiful in the evening as it was in the daytime. The streetlamps decorated with sprays of fresh flowers lined the sidewalk. Planters full of Sweet Peas, Marigolds, and Baby's Breath positioned between the lights created a fragrant pattern.

People nodded their greetings as Clark and Faith meandered down the sidewalk. Holly and Mischa were right, Faith decided. Paradise Hills had some magic in the air. Everything seemed lovely.

Faith lived three blocks from Main Street. It was close enough to make it safe to walk to the hub of the festivities but far enough to avoid the noise. The sun rested on the horizon's edge like a small child fighting for a couple more minutes to stay awake. She looked down at her walking tracker. It was close to 9:30.

Clark held her bags of conditioners and hair treatments and fell in step with Faith on the walk to her house. "Montana summers. They're my favorite season." His comment drew her attention to the sounds and smells around them. They were in the neighborhood, and the scenery had changed. Tall trees lined the sidewalks to create a canopy for them to walk beneath. The heat from the sun, combined with the moisture from the trees, gave off a scent that only came on a warm evening. Crickets hiding in flowerbeds chirped their good-night song.

Faith felt young and in love. Not that she was old, but she was wiser and knew better than to give in to the urge to soften her heart. Still, there was nothing wrong with acknowledging the stirrings. To keep herself from falling too far into the warmth in her heart, she reminded herself of the hours and weeks with Skye to heal the ache of loneliness.

Skye forced Faith to be still. In doing so, Faith found herself and never wanted to lose touch with that person again. She wasn't perfect. As a matter of fact, she was messy and clumsy and made more mistakes than she cared to admit. Even then, they were something she could lay claim to.

Her talk with Holly over the weekend had shown Faith that while she veered away from the optimistic side of things, she also hadn't chosen to remain in the sea of bitterness. Faith attributed her positive outlook on life to being around Holly, Liam, Mischa, and Kellen. They were kindhearted people who consistently expressed appreciation for each other. When Holly brought Faith into the fold, they extended the kindness to her. Her friends had the gift of ribbing someone for their shortcomings. But they did it in a way that made the person comfortable with being human.

Clark seemed comfortable walking beside her in companionable silence. Either he, too, was caught in his thoughts, or he was enjoying the calm that always came when the two of them were together. His voice sounded far away when he asked, "Remember when we were at 4H camp in junior high?"

Paradise Hills Summer

"Who could forget?" Faith replied, "That was when I fell in love with Montana summers."

They spent all day soaking in the sun. Even though the camp separated the boys from the girls, Clark always found his way to Faith.

He never pulled any pranks or did anything questionable. He simply wanted to do the activities with Faith. Midway through the week, the counselors gave up and included him in the group.

They canoed and swam. Clark helped Faith learn how to shoot a bow and arrow. He did so well that she won a blue ribbon at the camp competition at the end of the week.

"That was when I fell in love with you."

Faith turned and caught Clark's profile. He gazed at a clearing in the trees. She looked up to see what held his attention. Stars shimmered above them. One seemed to twinkle and return to the same level of brightness as all the ones that surrounded it.

Clark's confession opened Faith's eyes to their life through his eyes. He was always joining her friends to get closer to her.

It happened when they were children. That is how they reconnected.

Just this evening, they relived the same routine. She was with her friends. He joined the group and waited each one out until it was his turn to receive her attention.

Faith's throat tightened. *No wonder Clark thought her friends were always more important to her.*

The pain from the discovery pinched Faith so tightly, she forgot the tearful promise she made to herself as she pulled into Paradise Hills with the bed of her pickup full of her belongings. She promised never to be weak around Clark Grayson for as long as she lived.

125

Faith wriggled her hand in Clark's and gripped it. As she tightened her hold on the moment, she loosened the one she used to hold onto the pain and said, "That was the best summer ever."

22

WALK HOME

Faith Alexander had his heart. She always had.

Once upon a time, it scared Clark. The woman had the power to crush him. But she never exercised or wielded it over him.

Even when they were younger. When other children were loose with their words and often said mean things, Faith held her tongue.

Her strength became Clark's weakness. It was the things she hadn't told him that drew his concern, which made it all the harder to explain to his family why he reacted the way he had.

"Was Faith talking to another man?" his father asked.

At this point, the cloud of anger surrounding Clark made it nearly impossible for him to express himself. He hid within it shaking his head no.

That and he had no way of explaining that he didn't believe Faith loved him. Her disregard for his request validated it.

In Clark's mind, he could have handled the declination of his request. Not responding to it at all… How would they handle the other problems in their marriage? Push them under the rug? Pretend they didn't exist until they exploded.

That is precisely what happened. Clark exploded.

The physical pain from the accident and the tearing of his heart resulted in a mushroom cloud of emotion.

Even then, when Clark was at his worst, Faith was at her best. "I was willing to stand before God and our friends and family and promise to be there in sickness and health. I mean to hold up my end of the promise."

He heard two things: Friends before family and the absence of love. Faith hadn't said that she loved him. Which made Clark an obligation—not someone she wanted.

Clark gazed over at Faith. The moonlight illuminated her face. She grinned the way a woman did when she was pleased with a trip to the salon. He found himself captivated by the confidence she exuded. Did Faith know how beautiful she was? She had to have. That's probably why she could hold back her love. She was fully aware that he didn't deserve her love. Especially not now. They crossed the street to the next block.

Faith had changed since leaving the small town. She was strong-spirited then. Now she was an independent woman who knew what she wanted and what to do to gain it.

Clark chuckled to himself when recalling the incident with Faith and the skunk. It was true to her character to take the matter in stride.

People could find Faith purely by scent, and she was worried about cleaning the horse. Once Willie and Brad assured Faith they didn't want her help with the horse, she left alone to deal with the stink. The Faith from Castle Hill would have had an entourage to accompany her.

A family had gathered on the porch in one of the houses they walked by. The mom sat on the porch swing with a baby

Paradise Hills Summer

on her lap. A man who looked to be in his early thirties made funny noises to make the baby giggle. It was hard to tell who laughed harder, the wife or the baby. The scene contrasted where Clark was in his life. The man on the porch had everything Clark wanted.

What began as a mission to reconcile gradually changed course for Clark. Faith had every reason to write him off. He gave it to her.

She also had proven that she was better off without him. Maybe it was time for him to give up the fight. Clark tried and failed. It hurt, but it was a truth he could accept.

As they walked down the tree-lined streets of Paradise Hills, Clark allowed himself one last time to love Faith. He'd start at the beginning, and when he dropped her off at the door, it would be the end.

After they said goodnight, he'd take a page from Faith's book and have fun with his friends. Maybe he'd explore the countryside. Montana was larger than some countries. Yet, he had only adventured the lower quadrant of the state.

"Remember when we were at 4H Camp in junior high?" Clark was so enamored with Faith. He took every chance to be with her and made a couple of opportunities when he saw they would work.

Midway through the week, the counselors of the girl's cabins took Clark in as their mascot. Since he had their trust, he respected the well-laid boundaries.

Faith leaned her head back and smiled as the memories came to her. He saw it in the tilt of her lips. "That was the best summer ever."

It was the only summer they went to camp. The next year they both were in high school sports. They trained. As they walked in silence, the memories poured in. The proms, the

129

college parties, the squabbles, and the kisses when they made up. They had quite the history.

By the next block, Clark was ready to pull away and give Faith the room to bloom. Then the furthest thing from his mind happened. She placed her hand in his. The touch, soft yet subtle, pushed aside his initial concerns and reassured him. They were meant to be together. He didn't know how or when it would happen, just that it would.

They walked in companionable silence. Fearing he'd ruin the moment, Clark didn't speak. Time passed too quickly, and they were in front of Faith's house.

"Thank you for walking me home. I appreciate it." Faith kept her hand in his. Clark would not be the first to release his grip. He let go of her once. That was a mistake he'd never make again.

The moonlight reflected in Faith's eyes, and Clark fell deeper in love with her than he had been five minutes prior. The pain he caused reflected from the depth of her irises.

"I am so sorry." The apology came before Clark had time to think it through.

Faith blinked and softened her grip. Clark wasn't ready for her to pull away. He gripped her hand. "Don't leave yet. I have to say this." She tilted her head to let him know she was ready to hear what he had to say.

"I was in so much pain. I didn't know what I was doing."

Her brow wrinkled.

Clark's voice faltered, "I thought you didn't want me. Instead of asking and giving you a chance to explain, I went off the deep end." She cast her eyes down toward the ground. "My impulsiveness hurt you."

Her head bobbed to relay what he said had hit home. Faith regarded him with thoughtful eyes that somehow shielded what was going through her mind. A wistful smile formed on

Paradise Hills Summer

her lips. "I'm sorry too. I don't know what I could have done to change things. But I'm sorry things ended the way they did." She squeezed his hand, pulled it free, and turned toward the house.

Clark sighed as he watched Faith approach the front door of her house. She unlocked and opened it without as much of a glance back.

He turned to head back to where he had parked his car. Clark hadn't made it to the corner when he heard Faith. "Clark, you have my conditioner." The small bag hung off his wrist. He turned around to give it to her.

"Thank you." Faith's voice was breathy from hurrying. She wrapped her arms around him and squeezed his waist. The hug was so quick Clark didn't have time to process what happened before she released him and backed away. "Goodnight."

Clark reached for Faith's arm and caught her by the elbow. The gentle tug was enough to convince her to stop. He had waited for the chance to reconnect.

It was now or never.

He asked in a low composed voice, "When you close your eyes and imagine us, what do you see?"

"I don't." Faith shifted to walk away from him.

"You're a bad liar, Faith. You always have been." His voice rose slightly for emphasis. "I'll tell you my vision. It's you and me in the grocery store bickering over how to choose a cantaloupe. I say look for the bee sting in the skin. You say it's how the section where the vine separates from the fruit smells. Then we end up buying a pre-sliced half because neither of us knows who is right."

"What does cantaloupe have to do with...?"

"We've learned how to argue." Clark caressed Faith's elbow to entice her to move toward him. "It's time we learned how to make up. We're settling this once and for all."

Clark glided his hand down Faith's arm to connect with her hand. "You do not understand what you do to me."

Clark touched her chin with his other hand and leaned forward. Her body aligned with his, and she raised her chin to meet him. Their lips touched softly like a whisper in the quiet of the night.

He sensed her need to connect and pressed his lips into hers. Her body arched into him and ignited his deeper want of her.

Faith gasped and softened.

Clark wrapped his arms around her back and pulled her into him.

She touched his jaw with the back of her hand. It was the gentle invitation he had spent months waiting for.

His mouth covered hers hungrily.

She hummed a note of delight.

His eyes burned into her, and a tangle of emotion took over. Faith was his. This time nothing would come between them.

Clark pulled out of the kiss, and Faith gasped her complaint.

He whispered hoarsely, "Faith, I want to be with you."

She cupped his jaw with her hands and touched her lips to his. "You already are."

Determination to have what he wanted to be pushed through his desire to have her. Clark didn't want a fling. His eye was on something more substantial.

That day when they were nine years old, and he kissed her, he claimed her as his. They were too young, and Clark didn't have the vocabulary or the emotional intelligence to express it.

Paradise Hills Summer

But the intention was there. He almost blew it when he didn't ask her to the dance first.

When she disappeared from Castle Hill without a backward glance, Clark made a promise to himself. If he ever got a chance at the love he wanted, he'd do everything in his power to do it right.

His foolishness taught Faith to look for any signs of insincerity. Anything further than passionate kissing would provide kindling to her suspicions. She'd brush aside the connection as being a side effect of Liam and Holly's wedding. Nothing would happen until Faith was in their bed in their house as his wife.

Faith brushed her tongue along his lower lip, and Clark yielded to the kiss. He groaned. Partially in pain but mostly in pleasure.

The connection was still there. Then he slowly slid his lips away from hers. "Faith," the huskiness in his voice betrayed his will to present a controlled facade. "I have to go before we do something that will result in a smaller version of both of us."

"You're right." The moonlight accented the wistful expression on her face. "Then again, you always were. Goodnight for real this time, Clark."

He listened to the soft clack of her sandals on the cement as she headed down the path to her door. She turned to face him and smiled softly. Then, she waggled her fingers to bid him goodbye.

Clark remained in place until the door shut. He exhaled and reminded himself the minor losses were at the expense of the major gains.

23
CHECKING IN

Faith curled up on the corner of her couch for an early morning chat with her parents. Because all of the Alexanders worked early, four a.m. was the perfect time for a quick chat.

Using the position of the video screen for clues, Faith would have guessed that her father was sitting in his gray recliner in the living room. The front of his hair rose and leaned in a messy pile toward the left side of his head. The lines around his eyes told her he was happy to hear from her. "Good morning, sweetheart."

"Things are getting busy over here, and I wanted to talk to you before they got out of control." She couldn't tell her parents Liam and Holly's wedding was three days away, and the bridal party was in full preparation mode. They had plans to get together every night for the rest of the week.

"It may be I haven't had enough coffee." Her father picked up his cup and drank a gulp of coffee. "But I would swear your hair looks different." Mark Alexander's ability to detect minute changes in a person's appearance attributed to his success as a businessperson.

Paradise Hills Summer

A slight turn of the lip, undetectable to most, elicited a question of concern from Faith's father. Most people begged it off as fatigue or stress. Every once in a while, though, a person shared whatever burdened them.

After that, they'd stop by Mark's Feed Store store more frequently. People could get most items at a lower cost at the big-name store thirty miles down the road. They shopped at Mark's business because they knew he cared.

"I had an incident with a skunk," Faith admitted.

"And the smell was so bad it changed your hair color?" Her father's chest rose with his laughter at his joke.

Faith smiled. She loved her father. He had the gift of making people feel comfortable with themselves. She told him about the solution used to rid herself of the odor before adding, "I wasn't supposed to use it in my hair." For the time being, her once brown hair was ash blond.

His eyes widened in horror. "I bet that set you back a pretty penny. Do I need to transfer money into your account?"

"Thanks for the offer, but I got it, Dad," Faith replied. After her nightmare of an almost wedding, she promised herself she'd never take money from her parents. Relying on them was what created the mess.

Her mother's face slid into the screen beside her father's. "Take the money. He makes plenty."

"Maybe next time." Faith also learned there were better ways to tell her mother no.

"Have you talked to Clark lately?" The hopeful glint in her mother's eye warned Faith to be careful. He talked to her parents. Anything Faith said could and would be used to manipulate her.

"Yes, we've made peace with the situation." Faith wanted to keep the conversation on neutral territory.

"What's that supposed to mean?" Her mother asked.

"We talked about some miscommunication. Now that I have the full story, Clark's reaction is understandable."

Her mother persisted with the outcome she wanted. "Are you two back together?"

"I don't think that will happen, mom." Faith sighed in resignation. The kiss they shared kept her up half the night. But it was just that, a kiss. They knew how to connect. Staying together was what eluded them. "Too much has happened."

"But he apologized?" Her mother pleaded on Clark's behalf

"Yes, we both apologized," Faith replied. Her mother was too in tune with Clark.

"So, you'll give him a chance?"

"There is no chance. We're just friends."

"Leave the kids to solve their own problems," Faith's father fussed.

"I'm just a hopeful romantic," her mother turned to address her father. The gentleness in her mother's features had Faith forgiving her for interfering. Her mother had the best of intentions. Unfortunately, her tendency to control situations overrode the goodwill.

Her parent's life was simple and perfect. Her mother and father loved each other. They had for most of their life. Then they worked together to raise two children: Faith and her brother, Matthew. Somehow, they saved enough money to send both children to college.

Matthew moved to Billings while Faith returned home to a life she hoped would mirror her parents. Instead, life took a left turn when Faith expected the world to shift to the right.

Helping Holly with her wedding to Liam showed Faith what she envisioned was possible. For some reason, it wasn't meant for her.

Clark was an amazing man. He was kind, funny, and

Paradise Hills Summer

warm. His drive brought him success. Most people, after an accident, would have let their injuries take over their life. Not only had he used his injuries to better himself, but Clark also made lemonade out of lemons by taking what he learned and helping others.

"One of us needs to be, Mom." Faith repositioned herself on the couch. She wanted to enjoy the last minutes of the call with her parents. "What are your plans for the weekend?"

Her mother kissed her father on the cheek, said, "I'll let you two talk," and disappeared from the screen.

"We're going on a day trip to the river. I'm catching some fish, and your mother will explore like she always does."

Faith heard what her parents hadn't said. They hadn't mentioned who was going on the trip with them. Her parents always traveled in groups.

When they were younger, families paired or tripled up and made a day at the river. This way, the kids had plenty of friends to occupy their interest. The moms kept a watchful eye while chatting around the campground with solo cups full of homemade Sangria. If the dads caught enough fish, they'd have fresh fish with fruit and vegetable salads brought from home.

Suddenly Faith made the correlation between German potato salad and the day trips. Once, Clark's mother brought enough salad to feed an army. Faith asked about the absence of mayonnaises. Hope Grayson explained that mayonnaise brought the susceptibility of food poisoning. What she brought along reduced the chances of having their day ruined by digestive drama.

"I love summer." Faith let the omission drop. Her parents deserved to have a day without guilt. "I hope you have fun."

"You too, Sweetheart."

They ended the call with pleasantries, and Faith got ready

for the day. She admired her new hair color. The lighter shade pulled the color out of her cheeks and gave them a healthy glow.

An image of Clark kissing Faith flashed in her mind. Her cheeks pinked an added degree.

What was she thinking? It had been so easy to give in to how she felt about him. Truth be told, Faith missed loving Clark. They had more good moments than bad.

Clark had the gift of keeping a situation alive. A party would be on its last legs. Then Clark would ask a question that sparked a lively conversation. People connected. Invariably, they'd associate Clark with the bonding and always invite him back. Faith bet that was what kept his relationship with Liam active over the years.

Holly explained that Clark and Liam knew each other from outdoor excursions. Sometimes they hunted together. Others, they'd hike rough terrain for scouting excursions. Even when Clark hadn't looked fit, he had an active lifestyle. Now his body matched the image he projected, which made it all the harder for Faith to find fault with him. She thought back to his question. Was there anything she could change about him? It would be their last conversation.

People talk about life-changing within the snap of a finger. Because Clark assumed her love lacked sincerity, Faith was the outsider in Castle Hill. Sure, people would be polite, but she'd be a party to fragmented conversations. They'd change the subject as she approached groups. Or worse, they'd walk away to continue their conversation elsewhere.

Clark was right. The kiss was amazing. But it couldn't happen again. If it did, they'd be back to where they started. But this time, it would be worse; what was against them would always rob Faith of the contentment she saw in couples together under far more favorable circumstances.

24

YOU ARE RIGHT

*G*ibson's restaurant was on the edge of Paradise Hills. The mountain range at the edge of the town offered varying views depending on the sun and clouds.

Faith escaped the crowd by venturing to the outdoor patio and watching the clouds float across the sky. Tables were stationed around a large fire pit, but Faith sat at one closer to the railing. Off in the distance, a stream trickled through the Buffalo Berry bushes.

It was eight at night, but they still had two hours of sunlight. Faith tilted her face toward the sky to listen for signs of nature. A soft breeze tickled her hair. Otherwise, the joyful chatter dominated the environment. It was like nature wanted to absorb the joy of Holly and Liam's upcoming wedding too.

As the wedding date approached, Faith faded into the background. She became less of an adviser and more of an extra set of hands for Holly

From what Faith could tell by watching Liam and Holly, She'd say they would have a strong marriage. The adoration that filled Holly's eyes every time Liam walked into the room boasted her commitment to their future.

While Holly was reserved in her approach, Liam's presence filled the room. He didn't bask in the attention. Instead, he used his energy to pair people off. More than once, Faith heard his signature introduction of "You have to meet...."

The more she watched Liam, the more Faith realized that the "blind date" resulted from Liam's natural inclination, not Clark's manipulation of the situation. Clark swore it was a sign. Mischa dropped her conspiracy theory and sided with Clark. "I can't help it," Mischa blushed. "Since Kellen has been hanging out with Clark, he's more considerate."

It seemed like Clark also influenced Liam, who took more of an active role at the wedding since he heard the story of what went wrong with Clark and Faith. At the rehearsal, Liam repeated every instruction and confirmed it with Holly, verifying that they were on the same page.

Holly's father chose not to attend the wedding. While it disappointed Holly, her father's actions didn't surprise her. The Lane family took it all in stride and changed the theme. Instead of the father giving the bride away, the walk down the aisle symbolized Liam's father bringing Holly into the fold.

Faith flinched at the explanation. Holly and Liam's wedding was everything that her wedding to Clark lacked. Their families worked together to create the occasion.

Faith began to piece together that perhaps Clark's mother had interpreted Faith's way of handling her mother's temperament as shutting the Grayson family out of the planning. It was no wonder his family didn't want to have anything to do with Faith. Without throwing her mother under the bus, there was no way to remedy the situation.

Stella and Susan, Holly and Liam's mothers, came up alongside Faith and set their drinks on the railing separating the restaurant from the surrounding landscape. Liam's mother, Stella, wore a floral tea-length dress. Holly's mother, Susan,

Paradise Hills Summer

wore a long sleeve linen dress with long jewelry to dress up the outfit. Both women seemed content. Stella said, "I could never grow tired of this view."

"Who would have thought we'd be at a rehearsal dinner for our children?" Susan glowed. "If we tried to set them up, this never would have worked."

The gentle companionship the women exuded warmed Faith. She hoped she'd be like this with Holly and Mischa when they were older. Her mind invariably drifted toward Clark's and her mother. She didn't want to imagine the conversations they had about Clark and her. It probably went along the lines of criticizing Faith for abandoning the town where she had grown up.

But Faith hadn't abandoned them. She ran away from the pressure of their dreams for her life.

In her move to Paradise Hills, Faith learned to hope. She hoped to travel and try foods from around the world. Faith also hoped for relationships that would endure the trials of aging. Most important, she hoped to learn how to love herself unconditionally.

"How are you doing, Faith?" Susan regarded her with a soft concern.

Faith guessed Holly must have told her mother what happened between Clark and her. If someone had asked Faith the same question three months ago, she wouldn't have been comfortable answering the question. Yet, here she was, close to seven months after her fiasco of a wedding, relishing the experience as a bridesmaid. "I am impressed by all that you accomplished in six months."

"I think it's because we are teachers." Stella pushed on the lime in her drink with her straw. "We organize so many activities every year, it just becomes natural. Form a team of people who are good at what they do and let them shine."

Liam's older brother, Gibson, appeared from around the corner with a long-handled lighter. "I thought I'd start a fire and get more people out here."

Faith looked up from Gibson to catch Clark coming out the door. She inhaled in appreciation of how he looked in dress pants and an untucked long-sleeve shirt. It seemed like he grew more and more attractive as the days passed. She caught herself mid-appreciation. It was okay to admire him, but she was not allowed to do it to the point of attaching any desire to be with him. Although, the increasing chain of communication between them made the promise harder and harder to fulfill.

His eyes reflected an appreciation for the landscape behind her. The corners of his mouth curved slightly. "Sunrise or sunset?" Faith turned to admire the scene. The colors had changed in the short time she'd been out on the patio.

"Sunrise," Stella said, "with a cup of coffee."

"Sunset." Susan held up her glass. "With a sweet red wine."

"Ooh," the lines near Stella's eyes deepened. "I might want to change my mind."

"Why can't we like both?" Susan suggested. "Sometimes, a good beginning sets the tone for a good day. But I like happy endings too."

"I can agree with you," Clark spoke to what Susan said but kept his eyes on Faith. "What do you prefer?"

The question was loaded. Faith worried that her answer was an indictment of her character. Who didn't want a happy ending? What was the point of hardship if it didn't bring some sense of satisfaction at the end of it all? She deferred the question. "You tell me yours first."

"I'm not a morning person. My idea of a good day is snuggling in bed. It makes it a little difficult to see the sunrise."

Faith's heart quivered at the innuendo in his words. It

Paradise Hills Summer

seized at the realization that Clark might not mean her. Sure, they had talked a lot lately, but they had scars buried beneath the pleasantries. He was at peace with her now. What if she unknowingly said or did something that struck a tender chord and upset him? They would be back at square one with his mother, declaring she was right.

Stella piped in, "On that note, I think we need to refresh our drinks."

Liam and Holly's mothers directed Faith's attention to their surroundings. She shifted her focus to the voices behind them. The laughter and chatter from the banter seemed to beckon them.

Clark set his hand on top of Faith's. "What would you say if I told you I was in love with you, Faith Alexander?"

"I'd say I believe you," she flirted.

He smirked. "You wouldn't say you loved me?"

Faith blushed and looked away. She had made a promise to herself a few seconds ago. His sweet voice, combined with the clean scent of his cologne, rewired her intentions. The last thing she needed was for him to know she was one step away from asking him to take her back.

"Ha, you love me," Clark taunted like he had won a game. The playfulness in his voice erased the vulnerability that held her voice hostage.

"Why won't you tell me the truth."

His family hated her. They hadn't said it directly, but the last conversation set the tone for the future.

Faith didn't want to hurt Clark's feelings. They saw marriage through Liam and Holly's relationships. Clark and Faith's story was different. Her mother was controlling. His mother was a mover and shaker in her own right within Castle Hill. Disapproval from either was the kiss of death. Faith had garnered it from both. She'd never put herself in that position ever again.

"Because it won't work. We have too much against us."

"My temper?"

Before she lost the courage to say it, Faith blurted, "No, our parents."

Clark's lips formed a thin line. "It's crazy how you get it, but you don't. This is about you and me. Not them."

"You are irresistibly handsome." Faith took Clark's hand in hers. "Too handsome for my good. Which is why I've tried to keep up. But I'm tired, Clark. I'm not as strong, or as fast, or as smart as you." She echoed the messages delivered by both of their parents. "I'm not good enough."

Confusion removed the dark anger in his eyes.

She continued. "Feeling like a failure is awful." Until she fought to take in a breath, Faith hadn't known she was holding it in. Faith rubbed Clark's hand. "I love you. I always will. I love you enough to tell you it's time I let you go so you can find someone right for you." She forced herself to smile.

"How can I say it in a way you'll understand, Faith? I. Need. You. You are the first thing on my mind when I wake and the last thought before I drift off to sleep. When I start a project, I think about how you will be impressed. That it will prove I'm good enough for you. You make me want to be a better person." Clark's voice lowered to a pleading tone. "Faith. Please. Give me. Give us a chance."

"This isn't the time to talk about us. Holly and Liam are getting married tomorrow afternoon."

"Then give me a kiss and a hug, and promise me we will discuss this later." He held his arms open to draw her in. Faith obliged his request and walked into him.

Clark wrapped his arms around her. "I'll see you tomor-

Paradise Hills Summer

row." He kissed her on the top of her head. Then he tucked his finger under her chin and gave her a quick peck on the lips.

The familiarity of the warm gesture settled Faith's heart, which didn't make sense to Faith. They hadn't reached a conclusive end to their problem. She stepped away from Clark, and he released his hold. Like the pins in a lock, several small clicks dropped information into place.

Her brows furrowed as she processed the information.

She was looking for a neon sign when Clark had been dropping cookie crumbs of patience to lead her back to him.

The apology followed by daily visits to the kiosk for iced coffee.

The barrage of this or that questions because he wanted to know the "New Faith."

His declaration of love as a follow-up to her refusal to believe his intent.

The kiss that had her wishing they were back together.

A peacefulness settled in the newly opened space in Faith's heart. She didn't think. The words flowed as though the turmoil of the past year hadn't happened. She said, "I love you."

Then Clark replied, "That's what's kept me going all this time. "

25

FRIENDS

Liam's brothers, Mark and Hunter, stepped aside to make room for Faith to pass by them. She disappeared into the crowd. Hunter held a small glass with a caramel-colored drink. Clark would guess scotch or a whiskey on the rocks. Mark had a beer. "We are about to head to the hotel."

Clark had been familiar with the routine until this part of the wedding. He never made it this far.

Mark said, "We have the tuxedos."

Hunter added, "I have the decorations for the car in my trunk."

"The veggie and meat platters will be in the room when we arrive," Clark confirmed his role as groomsman. He made sure they ate healthily. Liam didn't want anybody at his wedding sick or hungover.

The men stayed in one wing of the resort while the women reserved a section of rooms on the other side. They assigned a team of bodyguards at either end of both wings. So far, mention of Liam and Holly's wedding hadn't made it to the media. Just in case someone had leaked the date or location,

Paradise Hills Summer

they had put safety measures in place. Toby, Kellen, and Liam joined them on the patio. "The rest of the guys are on their way to the resort."

Clark tied Liam's calm demeanor to his brothers. When his eyes darted back to the restaurant's interior, Hunter joked, "We already know Mom and Susan will not let you go anywhere near Holly until noon tomorrow." The warmth in Hunter's demeanor made Clark miss his brothers. They moved shortly after graduating college and returned for the occasional visit. Then it was a barrage of family members, eliminating moments to show closeness.

The men piled into Hunter's Suburban and headed to their rooms at the resort. Five miles into the drive, Kellen's phone flashed a notification. He checked the message, grinned, and typed his reply. Before he had time to place the phone in his pocket, another message came through. Kellen read the screen and chuckled. His fingers scrolled through an emoji, and he replied.

"What is the probability we'll be at Kellen's wedding next?" Mark's voice drew everyone's attention to the back seat.

"I'd place my money on you, Mark," Hunter answered. All the men turned to the front seat.

"Did you see Clark and Faith getting mushy on the patio?" Kellen goaded.

Toby, who sat beside Mark, said, "This is some great material for a song." He leaned to the side and pulled a notepad from his back pocket. "Y'all keep talking."

The men fell silent and turned to face the front.

Undeterred, Toby goaded, "I have enough to get started." From where he sat, Clark heard the pencil scratches gliding across the paper.

To avoid unnecessary attention, Hunter bypassed the front entrance of the resort. He took the route the employees used to leave via a road beside the golf course. From there, they passed by the stables. The horse Faith loved neighed a greeting as the Suburban passed by.

"You have yourself a little piece of heaven," Toby kept his eyes glued to the surrounding landscape. "I can see how it was so easy for you to leave California."

"Traffic jams are caused by herds of deer," Kellen boasted.

"It's funny. You came here for something smaller. I came here to get lost in the crowd." Clark mused, "Perspective dictates the interpretation of the situation."

They piled out of the car and formed smaller groups. Clark noticed that Mark was engrossed in a text conversation on his phone. If the upturned corners of his mouth were any sign, he was communicating with his girlfriend, Madison.

Kellen picked up where Clark had ended the conversation in the car. "What is your situation?"

"I don't follow," Clark was an open book with Kellen. There was no reason for him not to understand what was going on in his life.

"From the outside looking in, you and Faith are a great match. Mischa says since you've been in the picture, you're all Faith talks about."

Clark wanted to ask what Faith had said. Instead, he fought to keep his cool. She had gone from not mentioning him to talking about him all the time. He knew she was in love with him, but the distance she kept between them had him second-guessing. "She's everything to me."

"Then what's the problem?" Kellen's tone conveyed the sincerity behind his question.

"My mother." Clark rolled his eyes.

"Ouch," Kellen exhaled his sympathy.

"No, ouch. Why, ouch?" Clark didn't see the problem. His mother may have overstepped her bounds, but she apologized

Paradise Hills Summer

to him afterward. She went so far as to approach Faith's parents with him to explain why they behaved so poorly. Then she made amends with Faith's mother. His mother wasn't the problem. As far as he could tell, Faith just needed time to forgive her.

"Let me guess. You sided with your mother." Kellen's face was devoid of judgment, yet the curve on the right edge of his lip told Clark he was prepared to make a point.

"I didn't take sides." Faith didn't give Clark a chance. She left without a word.

"Did you have your mother apologize to Faith?" Kellen maintained a straight face. His voice had a hint of hope that Clark would give the correct response.

"It will happen in time." Clark's mother had apologized to Faith's mother. "Most likely, when we go back for Faith's birthday... That will give them the chance to make peace."

"Twenty bucks says Faith goes on a vacation for her birthday." Kellen reached in his pocket for the money. "It'll be a women's retreat."

Clark signaled to Kellen's cell phone. "Did Mischa say something?"

"You did. Women act like they're strong and can handle business. And don't get me wrong, they can. But they want to know we'll protect them. If Faith has to make peace with your mother, what does she need you for?"

Mark approached with his cell phone. "Sounds like the ladies are having fun."

"This is a guy's night." Toby walked ahead of the group to the bank of rooms.

"Spoken like a man who doesn't have a girlfriend," Liam joked.

The other men were texting so frequently with their significant others that Clark wanted to see if he accidentally turned off or set his phone to airplane mode. To distract himself, he wandered around their room. It had a large area in the middle with a sectional couch in front of a fireplace. A big screen TV was suspended from the ceiling. The remote controls to a gaming system were set in an oak box in the middle of the coffee table. They could see the sun dropping behind the mountain range in the distance through the open curtains. Four doors led to the entrance of four rooms. Between the sitting area and the four bedrooms, the men had more than enough space to wander.

He should have been appreciating the accommodations. Faith's lack of correspondence and Kellen's interpretation of events set Clark on edge.

In so many ways, Faith had said the same thing. That first time she saw him, she ran for cover. Mischa and Kellen guided her back to the restaurant. Then Mischa glared at him — like a scowl would scare him off.

When Faith had the tussle with the skunk, she turned to the old man who took care of the barns for help. How many times had their friends run interference for her? They inadvertently were giving Faith the message that Clark consistently did not deliver. She knew she was safe with them.

Clark and Faith were in the exact situation they ran away from. Their friends influenced their relationship. This time around, it didn't bother Clark. At last, Kellen explained why. Friends weren't there to interfere. They held up the end of the table he neglected to secure. While Clark appreciated the support, it bothered him. He wanted Faith's trust. More importantly, he wanted to be worthy of it.

26

THE SIGN

*H*olly and Liam's wedding had been a celebration of love. The fun in all the work manifested an experience they'd remember long after the last piece of wedding cake had been eaten.

The wedding party connected over projects that supported the community. They went on to reinforce the "we're working together on something important" vibe by helping with little tasks like wrapping ribbons around place markers. Who wouldn't want something like what they'd experienced over the past month as the start of a new life?

Awe. If Faith were to ascribe any emotion about the experience, she would have to say it was awe.

Everyone in the room gushed joyfully when Liam kissed Holly as his bride. Faith, who had lived vicariously through them, felt a sense of relief. Happily ever after existed.

The reception was a bigger whirlwind than the ceremony. The combination of Liam's Hollywood friends with his Paradise Hills family created a guest list larger than any group Faith had ever seen. And the dazzle. Everyone, the men included, was beautiful. It was as if someone had coated the guests with glossy paint. They seemed to sparkle.

People Faith had never met invited her into conversations about Paradise Hills and all that it offered as means of entertainment.

A slender man in a tailored suit caught her on her way to the ladies' room. "I meant to talk to you all afternoon. Do you have a minute?"

Faith threw a glance at the restroom. She couldn't tell if the small group of women outside the door was the beginning of a line, or if they had gathered for a mini-discussion. With her luck, it would be a line, and she'd look like she was avoiding him. "What did you need?"

He blinked, apparently taken aback by her question.

"You've been waiting to talk to me about…." Faith forced a grin to help him finish the sentence.

His lips formed the most charming smile she had ever seen. Faith's heart gushed—the way he made her feel. Faith understood the whole swooning thing. His voice turned to velvet. "I was hoping you'd have some time this weekend for dinner and to do something that would seem quaint to me but natural to you."

He sounded like one of the men on the BBC channel. Never in a million years. Faith never, in a million years, imagined a man who could have been James Bond would have asked her out to do something quaint.

Then he stiffened. The change in his affect was so sudden Faith turned to see what caused it. Clark had come up behind her. Faith stepped to the side to make room for him. She gestured with her hand, "Hey, this is." She blushed. While developing a crush, she forgot to ask the man's name.

"David." David's smile had cooled to polite.

Paradise Hills Summer

"Nice to meet you, David." Clark regarded him with a nod. "Do you mind if I pull Faith away for a sec?" He didn't give David or Faith a chance to reply. Clark took Faith by the hand and led her away from the pretty man. When they were out of hearing range, he stopped. "Holly is getting ready to throw the bouquet."

Why it mattered to Clark that Faith was there to catch the flowers made no sense to her. Faith glanced at David, who had his hand on his chin. He seemed amused by Clark's diversion. "I don't want to catch the flowers."

Clark threw a look at David. Faith compared the two men. In his groomsmen's blue tux, Clark looked handsome. Liam's stylist had parted his hair to the side and gelled it back. With his short beard, he was rugged compared to David, who was controlled. It was James Bond versus a Viking. Clark set his hands-on Faith's waist and gave her a quick peck on the cheek. "You stay here."

Shocked by Clark's show of affection, Faith froze in place. She watched Clark approach David. Clark had his hands crossed in front of him like he was talking amicably with a friend. David looked at Faith over Clark's shoulder, and Faith sighed. Clark was chasing him away. It was the first time anyone attractive had paid her any attention. Recalling how she ended up in the alcove, Faith checked the door to the ladies' room. The line had shrunk, so she made her way to the bathroom.

The women she saw earlier were checking their lipstick in front of the mirror. Before Faith knew it, she had joined their conversation. Faith wasn't in the bathroom for long, just long enough to build a rapport with the women she hadn't met before the wedding. They left the bathroom, chatting away like they had known each other for longer than five minutes.

Clark leaned against the wall while he waited for her at the end of the alcove. He straightened when he saw her. "We need to talk."

How was it that four words could touch on so many emotions? Was Clark angry with her? Had something happened, and he was the bearer of bad news?

Faith searched for an excuse to avoid "the talk." Nobody was around them. "Ah, sure. What about?"

"Are you avoiding me?"

Faith searched Clark's eyes for the root of his question while her heart contracted in fear of him seeing the struggle within her. She was beyond happy for Holly and Liam. Yet, beneath the elation, Faith mourned the marriage she'd never have.

"I want to be there for you." The warmth in Clark's voice pleaded for the chance Faith never offered.

"You are here," Faith replied. "We've been together all day." They took pictures together and danced. When the intensity of the day had grown to be too much, Faith receded from the group. But she returned after the momentary breaks. Kind of like she was doing now.

The want in Clark's eyes drew her to him. "You came to me when I was at my lowest. You stuck with me when I didn't deserve it."

A soft gasp escaped from Faith's mouth. She placed her hand over her lips to prevent herself from giving any other response.

Clark rushed to her and kissed her like it was the last kiss they'd ever share. The raw emotion passed through his touch to strike her heart before Faith had time to guard it. Faith hummed her approval. Clark cupped her chin and pressed his lips into her, forcing them to open. His claim set her body on fire. With her yield, she saw swirls of red and orange in her mind. He pulled away suddenly, and Faith drew in a deep

Paradise Hills Summer

breath. Clark's lips were swollen from their kiss. His eyes bore into her. "I loved you when we were children. I love you now, and I want to love you when we are old and gray."

Faith gulped. Clark's declaration left no room for interpretation. They hadn't finished what they started when he kissed her on that rock when they were nine years old. She cleared her throat. "I love you, too." What that meant in the big picture didn't matter. Clark wanted to be with her. And despite all they had been through, Faith wanted to be with him too.

Clark took her hand in his. "Now, let's go have some fun."

"We were having fun back there," Faith gestured with her hand to the place where Clark kissed her.

Kellen hurried to Clark and pulled him to the side. Clark ran his thumb along the bottom of his lip, and both men chuckled. Leaving Clark with a pat on the back, Kellen resumed his course to what Faith assumed was the bar for another beer.

Mischa stopped short in front of Clark and Faith. A sly grin crossed her face. She tilted her head toward the front of the room. "They're getting ready to throw the bouquet. Can you do me a favor and push me out of the way if it comes near me?" To Faith's questioning glance, she added, "I don't need the pressure. Kellen and I just started dating. I like where we are." Then she said, "Based on the matching lipstick, I'd say you two are closer to "I do" than Kellen and me."

Faith's cheeks reddened. She swirled to return to the restroom to freshen her makeup. "You can get pretty in just a minute." The women had assembled in front of Holly. Mischa hurried to join the group. Faith slowed to a turtle's pace. She didn't want the pressure of a wedding either. The last time she tried, she failed. She lingered toward the outskirts of the group to ensure she did not catch the bouquet.

Holly launched the bouquet over her head. It arched, and,

155

MERRI MAYWETHER

to anyone observing, it looked like some lucky woman in the middle of the cluster would catch it.

The spray of burgundy, periwinkle blue, and white flowers bounced off a woman's hand. Another woman swiped at it, sending the array of flowers back into the air. Suddenly the world moved in slow motion.

Faith saw the flowers arch over the heads of the women. It went higher than the initial throw. Women squealed and shifted to match the new trajectory. The next thing Faith knew, the wedding bouquet hit her square in the chest. Faith pressed her hand to her chest to keep it from falling.

The women she befriended in the bathroom clapped. One said, "Good for you."

The other said, "I'd say that guy she was kissing back there is off the market."

Mischa rushed to Faith's side and beamed. "Thank you for taking the hit for the team."

Echoes of the conversation in the hair salon came to her mind.

"Focus," Mischa snapped her fingers in front of Faith's face. "Signs. We're looking for signs."

"Signs of what?"

"A sign that proves you are destined to be together."

They were in Paradise Hills, where people looked for and believed in signs. The magic of Paradise Hills gave her an undeniable sign. The next one to get married was the one who caught the bridal bouquet. Faith's heart didn't seize with the pressure. Instead, it expanded with the sense of peace that filled her. She searched for Clark at the back of the room. Kellen and Toby were with him, and all three laughed congenially. When her eyes connected with his, a broad smile crossed his face. He winked and blew her a kiss.

156

27

SOMEONE IS PERKY

Refreshed from the recovery time on Sunday, Faith returned to work with a whistle in her song and a hop in her step...or something to that effect. She practically bounced as she set out the red, white, and blue Americana decorations for the upcoming Independence Day celebrations. "I bet the watermelon tea will be a hit. I love watermelon."

For some reason, Faith loved a lot about life. It was like someone had pressed a reset button and had given her a new perspective.

"Somebody's awful perky," Misty teased.

"I love weddings." Faith poured the water into the coffee pot. "They bring out the best in everybody." It certainly had for Clark. When they lived in Castle Hill, Clark preferred hanging out with the guys and having a beer in the corner.

He started the same way at Holly and Liam's wedding. Then he cornered her and kissed her. Faith's body burned every time she recalled the kiss. "I danced enough to burn off three weeks' worth of brownies."

Somehow information had been leaked that Liam and

Holly's wedding was in Missoula. The mystery was solved when Liam and Holly reserved a bank of luxury tents at Paws Up in Missoula, Montana. In passing, as he distributed the envelopes, Liam mentioned, "I may have let it slip at a press junket that I planned to have a fishing excursion with my friends."

Clark side-eyed Faith and Mischa when they opened the envelopes with the itinerary. "Are you sure you're not trying to avoid going home to Castle Hill for your birthday?"

"Yes, Clark, you have figured us out. Mischa and I hacked Holly's computer and got an expensive reservation. All so I could avoid my mother." She loved her mother. She loved her best when she was one hundred miles away.

Faith froze when she heard her mother's voice. "This is going to be so much fun."

"Did you know they had a big wedding here this week-end?" The other woman's voice chilled Faith's heart. Faith inhaled a deep breath. It couldn't be who she thought it was. Slowly she pivoted to see the guests, who sounded exactly like her mother and Clark's mother.

When she turned around and saw it was them, the warm fuzzy sensation was replaced by the vibrations, one would imagine feeling if they were on the inside of a bell. Faith forced what she hoped looked like a smile. "Mom. Betsy. What a surprise."

Misty's eyes darted back and forth from Faith to her mother and back to Faith. She said, "You have the same chin and nose as your mother." She scowled at Betsy. "It's probably the facial hair. Clark doesn't look anything like you."

How Misty knew Betsy was Clark's mother eluded Faith. She probably guessed from all the conversations that the women, who were best friends, would travel together.

Paradise Hills Summer

Betsy's new dark-rimmed glasses accented by her gray angular bob added a degree of spunk to her persona. Clark's mother always had a hint of sass in her voice that added humor or emphasis to what she said. Having been on the receiving end of both sides of her attitude, Faith would have preferred to avoid her altogether.

Her mother used a barrette to pull her shoulder-length hair away from her face. She had clasped her sunglasses to the front of her shirt. "After thirty-five years of marriage, I have decided that camping is not my thing."

"While the scenery is beautiful. The water is cold. Cold water messes with my arthritis." Betsy waved her hand dismissively. "And then, they expect us to cook and clean. I can do that at my house with heated water and sleep in my comfortable bed."

Faith didn't want to ask why they were at the Paradise Hills resort. But she wanted to know. Why were her mother and Clark's mother in front of the coffee kiosk complaining about their arthritis and cold water? The words came out of her mouth as she formed the question. "You came to Paradise Hills for a cup of coffee?"

"No. We came for a woman's retreat." Her mother sounded like the answer was obvious.

Faith's pep popped. She didn't know what was entailed in the woman's retreat. The anticipation in her mother's smile hinted that it included her. "Oh. That sounds wonderful."

Betsy cleared her throat. "We thought you kids might want to have dinner with us or hang out around the pool."

Faith didn't want to jump to conclusions. But it looked like Clark had set her up. He reeled her in with sweet gestures. The quiet evenings watching the sunset. The walks down Main Street, where they'd stop for ice cream or candy. He texted her that morning with a good morning, beautiful message. He proved that love was trustworthy. Then when she fell for it hook, line, and sinker, his mother smacked her over the head with the reality of their situation.

She didn't care how good it felt when he kissed her. Faith wasn't in the mood to swim in the pond with a shark. She would say as much when the pain of Betsy's harsh words struck her. Faith promised she'd never treat someone as poorly as she had been treated. She wilted when she said, "I'm sure we could come up with something." That was just as bad. She was back to being the people pleaser that got her pulled into the fiasco in the first place.

Misty nudged Faith to make room at the counter. "Can I get you something to drink? It's on the house."

Betsy glanced at Faith's mother. Hope wrapped her arm around Betsy's shoulder and gently squeezed it. Her smile said something to the effect of, "See, I told you it would be okay." Betsy tilted her head toward Hope, and half smiled.

Hope spoke. "We just wanted to stop by to let you know we're here. We'll catch up with you later."

The uncertainty in Betsy's eyes softened Faith's heart. There was more going on than Faith could decipher in the brief conversation. Faith said, "I'll call you as soon as I finish my shift."

Both women walked away, and the couple behind them stepped forward in line. From there, a constant stream of people visited the kiosk, making it difficult for Faith and Misty to talk about what transpired in the early hours of the day. Even more surprising was the absence of Clark's daily 10:00 visit. Since reconnecting with Faith, he stopped by every day for a small black coffee.

Faith guessed that his mother had got a hold of him. She

Paradise Hills Summer

wished she could be a fly on the wall to hear the conversation. The way Betsy interacted with her mother hinted at remorse— or could it have been nerves at seeing Faith again?

She took out the broom and swept the area around them. For some reason, a few grains of coffee wouldn't go in the dustpan. Faith swiped at them with a little more force, yet they remained in place.

The grounds were representative of what happened earlier in the day. It was like Betsy and her mother taunted her. Faith disdained being right. She told Clark that their mothers would interfere with their relationship. What were the odds they'd show up the day after Clark and Faith committed to giving their relationship another try?

"Let me have that, Broom Hilda." Misty eased the broom out of Faith's grip. "Why don't you head to the gym and have a chat with your Romeo?"

Just then, Susan, the hotel manager, stopped by the kiosk with a spray of flowers. "These are for you." She pulled the card out of the holder and handed it to Faith. The sender wanted me to make sure you received the note. The tender glint in her eye said she knew Clark's side of the story.

"Thank you," Faith set the flowers on the edge of the counter where people picked up their coffee. She was sure they'd enjoy seeing the flowers as much as she did.

Susan waited at the edge. "Are you going to read the note?" She smiled. "I'm supposed to report back that you read it."

The card was the size of Faith's palm. It couldn't have said much. She broke the seal with a stir stick and pulled out the note. In a font that resembled a typewriter stroke, it read, "I loved you yesterday. I love you today. I'll love you when I'm old and gray."

161

Faith read it aloud for Susan and Misty. "Oh," Misty gushed. "Now, you have to go and see him."

"He took off the afternoon," Susan said. "He said something about a surprise visit from his mother."

Faith's distress turned to concern. Clark was just as surprised by their mother's visit as she was.

28

PROPERTY OF 406

Clark slept in an hour. The night prior, he and Faith were up late talking, kissing, and canoodling. Somewhere between the kisses, he got her to agree to give them another chance.

The extra sleep and the recollection of Faith's affection had him walking on air.

Then he saw the equivalent of a summer blizzard at the entrance of the fitness center.

His mom, with her best friend Hope Alexander, were reading through the brochures on the door.

"Mom?" Even though she was standing there in front of him wearing her favorite "Property of 406" t-shirt and capris, Clark couldn't believe his mother was at his job.

Are you kidding me?

What were the odds? The day after, he secured Faith's trust, not one but both of their mothers made a surprise appearance.

"See, Betsy, I told you the kids would be happy to see us." Faith's mother sounded more confident than she looked. The waver in her voice gave away that the smile she presented was all show.

It was better than the cool undertones Clark learned were a false calm. Hope Alexander had something under her hat.

Clark ignored Hope and held out his arms to hug his mother. Her head landed at the top of his chest, so he curled around her to blanket her with affection.

"What brings you one hundred miles away from home?" He glared at Hope and quickly adjusted his expression to a smile for his mother.

"Well, we were on a camping trip with your father and John." She gestured toward Hope to show him who made up the other part of we. "Then, Matthew, Greg, and Colter arrived. It was five men and two women. That may be some woman's dream of fun, but taking care of five grown men while sleeping on rocks and bathing in ice water isn't my cup of tea anymore."

Hope nodded her agreement. "Then we got to thinking. There is a perfectly good resort a little more than an hour away. The men can have their fun, and we can have ours."

"I'm looking forward to having a drink with an umbrella in it." His mother clapped her hands softly in front of her.

"You're here in the resort where Faith and I work for a woman's retreat?" He didn't mean to sound cautious, but their story seemed a little suspicious.

"Why else would we be here?"

His mother had caught the tone. Clark had to think quickly. "How about I take off the day and spend the afternoon with you?" He had to update his mother on the progress between Faith and him. He also wanted to give Faith the chance to tell her mother.

Then it dawned on him. The two people that kept them apart had visited the resort because the convergence of the rest

Paradise Hills Summer

of the family drove them nuts. In his family, going nuts was like a cold. Once a person caught it, they felt the need to pass the discomfort on to the next person.

"I'd love that. We already visited Faith and told her we wanted to meet for dinner. We'll have a chance to catch up." Hope was too confident. Clark fell for her shenanigans once before, and it cost him his marriage to her daughter.

The weekend had been a crash course on navigating relationships, beginning with an introduction from Kellen, who had experience with overzealous parents. Then it progressed to Liam's brothers warning him about guarding his position with Faith.

Several men had stepped in line for the chance to catch Faith's eye. The first time Clark lost sight of her, one tried luring her in.

Clark did not spend the past twenty-five years of his life building a relationship with the woman to have it taken away without a fight. Even if it meant having words, respectful ones, of course, with her mother, he would remain within Faith's good favor.

He had to talk to the moms individually if he wanted to present his case. "Mom, could I have some time alone with you? We could have coffee and a danish in the hotel restaurant."

"I could go for a danish," Hope brightened.

Clark stretched his lips and bobbed his head to reduce the awkwardness of the situation. "I was aiming for a mother and son talk. You can join up with us afterward."

Hope's mouth widened with her, "Oh. Sure. I could go back to the room and unpack my toiletries… and watch some Good Morning America."

"Thanks, I need to talk to some people, and I'll be right there."

165

His mother patted him on the cheek before heading to the cafe.

Susan, the hotel manager, had an office beside Clark's. They had lunch meetings a couple of times a week, so she was aware of Clark's life before Paradise Hills. He tapped on her door and gave her the reader's digest update before explaining why he was taking off the day. When he gave her all the details, she rubbed the top of her brow. "Tell me you're sending Faith flowers."

"Ah, I don't have good luck with flowers. They send the wrong message."

"I'll make sure she gets the message." Susan slid an index card across the desk. "Write what you want to say, and I'll take care of the rest."

Clark found it odd that his boss was helping him with his relationship with Faith. He had to ask. "Why are you helping me?"

She grinned thoughtfully. "I was the one who hired Faith all those months ago. When she first got here, Faith was friendly and professional. But all of us could see something was missing. Then you arrived, and the metaphorical flower bloomed. It's obvious to anyone with eyes you two belong together. You know we believe in the magic of love in Paradise Hills. And, there is nothing we love more than a happily ever after." She winked. "If you have your wedding at the resort, it's a double win for us. We can use your wedding for promotional material."

While her words encouraged Clark, he didn't want to get his hopes too high. Experience taught him that until Faith had his last name, a lot could go wrong. "Thanks for the vote of confidence, but let's not put the cart before the horse."

Susan's eyes sparkled. "I cannot wait to say I told you so."

Paradise Hills Summer

CLARK'S MOTHER chose a seat in front of the floor-to-ceiling window. From his view at the entrance of the Paradise Hills Terrace, it looked like she was admiring the garden on the other side of the window.

One of the guests at the tables recognized him from the gym and discreetly greeted him with a wave. Clark nodded hello and made his way through the maze of tables to where his mother waited. He remained quiet when sitting across from her at the table to give her a couple more moments of peace.

Before he was fully seated, she said, "I know."

When he was younger, Clark believed his mother had a sixth sense. As an adult, he realized her secret was vague statements. I know said so much, yet so little. He always assumed she knew what he was trying to hide. When she said something as simple as "I know," she meant, "we need to talk."

He asked, "What do you know?"

"It's time to make peace with Faith." Her fingers fiddled with the red cloth napkin. "I don't know why I waited so long."

"She changed her phone number," Clark offered her room for justification. By the time they saw the full picture, Faith had moved. Clark assumed she wasn't responding to his texts because she was angry. When he heard the disconnect message, he realized the full extent of the damage. He heard through the grapevine that people had given her a hard time, and she moved. By then, his mother was horrified. There was no way for her to apologize without going through Hope.

Hope feared sharing Faith's personal information would be the straw that broke the camel's back. As it was, Faith kept her and the family at arm's length. Adding Betsy to the equation might have been enough for Faith to write off the whole Alexander clan.

"I could have written her a note." Betsy grinned wryly at the irony of her statement. It was a note that got them in trouble in the first place.

Clark reached across the table for his mother's hand. "Promise you won't be mad when I tell you what I'm about to tell you."

She squeezed it gently. "After what we've been through, I don't think anything could drive a wedge between us."

Clark took in a breath. With his exhalation, he replied. "Faith is giving us another chance."

His mother's eyes searched his face. "You're back together. Everything is fine?" After seeing Clark's frown, she murmured, "But it isn't."

"She's worried you'll come between us."

"Her mother goes to great lengths to control everything Faith does — down to the color of underwear she chose, and Faith is worried about me? That isn't fair."

"Not that I agree with Hope," Clark began. "In her dysfunctional way, she was trying to help Faith make me happy."

"But I'm your mother," Betsy pleaded.

The conversation hurt Clark. Because of his lack of foresight, his mother looked like the villain in the story of Clark and soon-to-be Faith Grayson.

Clark's mother was the most supportive person he knew. Betsy Grayson would walk on water for a person. "I'm not sending you away. I'm saying we need to understand Faith will need time to trust we're not against her—that we're here to build her up, not tear her down. It will take more than an apology to fix things."

Paradise Hills Summer

The server approached the table. "Welcome to the Paradise Hills Terrace. What could I get you this morning?"

Clark's mother cast him a questioning glance. "Are we done with our talk?"

Clark nodded.

Betsy said, "I'd like to order two cups of coffee?"

She responded to Clark's head tilt and eyebrow raise, "Do you really believe Hope will stay in the room to watch Good Morning America?"

As if on cue, Faith's mother appeared at the entrance of the restaurant. Her eyes begged for an invitation to the table.

Clark smirked and rolled his eyes. Faith's mother may have had boundary issues, but everyone knew she only had them with those closest to her heart.

29
INSTAGRAM

Clark's text came first. "Everything will be fine." Faith's eye twitched. That was easy for him to say. The mothers loved Clark. It was Faith who drew their scrutiny. Ire seeped through her body. She was not looking forward to dinner. He sent a follow-up message, "Have I told you I love you? Thank you for giving us a second chance."

Within seconds, a different one came from Faith's mother, "Looking forward to having dinner with my favorite daughter."

Faith quickly replied, "I am your only daughter."

"I know. But if I were to have more than one, you would be my favorite." Her mother punctuated the text with a winky emoji.

The three of them talked. They had to have. Her Castle Hill family never sent encouraging messages. Their text usually read something like, "What are we doing for dinner?"

Conversely, her text correspondence with her friends from Paradise Hills varied and was more frequent. Sometimes they communicated pertinent information like dates, times, and questions to help coordinate plans. Most of their daily texts

Paradise Hills Summer

comprised funny memes, "I appreciate you" posts, and quick updates on their day. Holly and Liam, on their honeymoon, had sent three different group texts by noon to let people know how great their first day of marriage had been.

Faith suspected coaching on behalf of Liam and Kellen had taken place. And it began sometime Friday night before the wedding, starting with a "Goodnight, beautiful" message from Clark. It worked. She drifted off to sleep, grinning like a schoolgirl.

While she liked the attention from Clark, the change in Hope Alexander set Faith on edge. A difference in perception didn't change a person's intent. Faith didn't know what it was, but the moms were up to something.

She tried piecing together information on her walk to the cafe where they planned to meet. Her mother was confident. Betsy seemed anxious. Since the wedding, Clark's message had been clear. He would prove that despite the detours, the signs pointed toward Faith and Clark going forward as a couple.

As soon as she opened the door to the cafe, Faith noticed the changes from the last time she ate at the restaurant. Little vases with sunflowers accented with red, white, or blue raffia replaced the pink carnations from the week prior.

Clark and the moms had arrived and were seated at a small table for four in the middle of the restaurant. Her mother had her hair pulled back with a star-spangled headband that matched her oversized top.

Betsy Grayson wore a tunic accented with alternating patterns of stars and stripes. Faith didn't know whether to stand and say the Pledge of Allegiance or go home and change into an outfit that matched their theme. She wore a simple taupe-colored tunic dress with brown leather strappy sandals. She did not fit in with them. The longer she was away from them, the clearer it became. No wonder they gave her such a hard time. They probably knew it all along and were trying to mold her to fit the image. Faith groaned inwardly. Dinner was going to be painful.

"You look amazing." Clark rose and came around the table to greet Faith. He took her hand and ushered her to the empty seat beside him. Like Faith, he wore neutral colors of khaki cargo shorts and a white v-neck t-shirt. Faith stole a glance at his backside and tightened her cheeks to hold in her appreciative grin.

When Faith motioned to reach for her seat, Clark rushed to beat her to it and pulled out the chair for her. The gesture caught Faith off guard. Her mind tilted. It was as though someone had adjusted her world by several degrees, and she hadn't made the matching adaptations. "Ah, thank you." She sat in the chair and set her purse strap on the back.

"I can see why you love it here," her mother gushed. "Paradise Hills is beautiful, and the people are so kind."

Faith smiled her agreement. She worried that anything she said would be perceived as a strike against Castle Hill. Before circumstances compelled her to look elsewhere, Faith loved Castle Hill. She didn't want her mother to think she left home for something better. "Did you have time to visit the pool?"

"As a matter of fact, I did," her mother replied. "And you wouldn't believe what I heard."

Faith didn't ask. Her mother would tell with or without an inquiry.

Sure enough, she followed with, "Your friends Liam and Holly had a large wedding at the resort this weekend."

Betsy's keys fell to the floor. Clark and Betsy both bent over to retrieve them. Introducing the topic of weddings made three of the four people uncomfortable.

Before the wedding, people kept silent about the ceremony

Paradise Hills Summer

to ward off unwanted guests and paparazzi. When Holly and Liam pulled away from the hotel in an inconspicuous Buick Regal to head to their honeymoon, everyone, the bride and groom included, filled their Instagram feed with a flurry of updates and well wishes for the newlyweds. Now that all the festivities were public knowledge, Faith felt comfortable sharing basic information. "It was a beautiful event."

"Too bad I had to hear about it from a stranger." Faith could tell things would head south quickly by the tone her mother used. Her mind raced to determine the direction the conversation was taking. If Faith could get one step ahead of her mother, she could divert and bring things to safer topics.

"You didn't give Faith a chance to say anything. She's been here for less than two minutes."

Faith's head jerked. Was that Betsy's soft voice coming to her defense?

Sure enough, Clark's mother showed her displeased half frown.

Faith had seen it several times over the years. When she and Clark stayed out too late or when she let a special word slip in the middle of a conversation. Never in a million years had she imagined her mother would be the recipient of the Betsy Grayson half frown of disapproval. What had happened since she left Castle Hill?

Hope tried justifying her question. "What mother wants to hear that her daughter was at the wedding of a lifetime from social media?"

"My mom is right," Clark joined the conversation. "Give Faith a break."

Her mother sighed. "Things were different when you lived in Castle Hill. We were like best friends, Faith. You told me everything. Now you've moved away, and I feel like I've lost a piece of myself."

The server came to the table and set a glass of water in front of Faith. "Can I get you something?"

Faith had never been so thankful for the interruption. Everyone shared their order and handed in the menus. When the server walked away, Clark picked up the conversation. "Look, this was supposed to be a pleasant meal where we reconnected and caught up on what has happened in the past few months. Let's continue with that in mind."

Had she heard correctly? Had her mother come out of her shell to show the controlling side of her personality? Had Clark taken command of the conversation? It was like moving one hundred miles to the north had created a polar shift.

Clark continued the conversation as though the interruption had never taken place. "Mom, what's been happening at the house?"

"We've made some changes." Betsy turned and pulled an envelope out of her purse. She slid it across the table toward Faith. "This is for you."

Faith wanted to ask, "What is it with the Grayson family and their tendency toward passing written notes." Instead, she glanced at Clark and begged him with her eyes to tell her what was happening.

His stretched lips said he didn't know.

When Faith picked up the envelope, Betsy answered her question. "We've had a lot of time to think. Marriage stretches a family. Roles change, and people learn to embrace unfamiliar personalities." She nudged her head towards Hope. "We both know you are a control freak."

Hope's mouth dropped.

Grace held up her hand to hold off the rebuttal. "But that is good. Your organizational skills and my creativity make us a dynamic duo."

She gestured toward Faith. "I made the mistake of

Paradise Hills Summer

ascribing your mother's personality to you. In my mind, you were controlling and had to do things your way. I have never been so wrong. You are flexible. We saw it when my son stuck his foot in his mouth. You didn't place stipulations on your support. You just gave it." She folded her hand in front of her and leaned forward for emphasis. "Because I saw you as your mother... and listened to my fool-headed son, who can be just as intense, I did not treat you like family. If that wasn't bad enough, I took their advice and gave you space when I should have pulled you into the fold. A million apologies cannot erase my contribution to your heartache."

Faith's throat clenched. She would have sworn Betsy Grayson hated her. She sniffed to blink away the tears. Clark took her hand in his.

"This is my peace offering to you. Please accept it with my apologies."

"What is it?" Faith's mother bounced her attention between Faith and Betsy.

Clark loosened his grip on her hand to give Faith the freedom to open the envelope. She turned open the top and pulled out an index card with cursive writing. The heading read, "Grandma Grayson's Potato Salad."

Faith squeaked and then threw a hand over her mouth to stifle the sound.

"What is it?" Her mother tilted in her seat to get a better perspective. Her jaw dropped. "Is that what I think it is?"

"It's a family secret," Betsy whispered. "I planned to pass it on to you much later than now." She looked a little chagrined when she asked, "Can you not use it in the county fair until after I go to the great beyond?"

When Faith left Castle Hill, she promised herself she'd allow no one from her hometown close to her heart ever again.

175

At the time, she thought it would be an easy enough promise to keep.

Everyone was clear about their opinion of her. Faith was synonymous with trouble. Most people rejoice when trouble goes running the other way.

Yet, those who told her she didn't belong went above and beyond. They apologized and took it a step further by proving they wanted her to be a part of their lives.

Faith's mother learned to express remorse for being too harsh. She also had developed the gift of using an explanation to soften her strong-arm tactics. Clark and Betsy had taken Faith's side against her mother.

If Faith were to use one word to describe what she felt, she would have to say it was overwhelmed. After that, it would be humbled.

She slowly rose from her seat. Her three deep inhalations were not enough to hold back the floodgate of tears. Through the gaps, she stuttered, "Thank you." Then she ran to the same bathroom where she tried to hide from Clark when she saw him weeks ago.

Before the bathroom door closed behind her, she heard Clark announce to the restaurant. "She's happy. My mother just gave her the family recipe for potato salad."

Faith sat on the stall and released the heart-wrenching cries she had held in for eight months. It wasn't a cry as much as deep inhalations and exhalations followed by an outpouring of tears. She cried over the loss of her special day. The memory of all the lonely nights when she scolded herself for being a fool piled on top of the pain.

The hinges creaked to announce someone else had entered the bathroom. "Faith? It's me. Mom. What's going on?"

Faith cleared her throat. "Nothing. I'll be okay in a minute."

Paradise Hills Summer

"Faith Alexander! Did you just nothing, your mother?" Her voice muffled as she turned to speak to someone. "She just nothing'd me."

"Give her a break, Hope. Clearly, she understands the power of the Grayson potato salad."

The argument between the moms struck Faith as humorous. Hope and Betsy were the perfect balance for each other. It was no wonder Faith and Clark connected. They were extensions of the best friends.

She used the back of her hand to wipe away her tears. When that didn't work, she pulled off a long roll of toilet paper and used it to dab under her eyes.

Betsy and her mother greeted her on the other side of the stall with eyes softened with concern.

Faith sniffled. "I'm sorry. I feel bad."

Both the moms frowned. "About?" Her mother asked the one-word question that had so many answers.

"I could have tried harder to get you to listen to me." She knew now if she had mentioned how her mother took over the wedding, Betsy would have supported Faith. Clark's mother had a way of talking to Faith's mother that made her listen to reason. But Faith wasn't about to throw her mother under the bus.

Hope wrapped an arm around Faith's shoulder. "That's all in the past. I promise I won't interfere with the next wedding."

"There's no next wedding." Faith and Clark had just agreed to try again. She didn't think she had it in her to organize another wedding.

"Of course, there is." Her mother placed her other hand on Betsy's shoulder to connect the three women. Betsy just gave you the Grayson family blessing."

"I don't know if I'm cut out for marriage, mom. When things got intense, I failed miserably."

177

"Clark," her mother singsong called through the door. She opened it to reveal him standing on the other side. Hope took Faith by the hand, dragged her to Clark, and made them connect. "You take over. I'm not blowing it for you again."

The moms sidestepped around Clark and Faith and hustled to their seats. Clark watched them disappear around the corner.

When they were out of sight, he opened his arms to hug Faith and pulled her in. His touch comforted her better than anything he could have said. In the silence, she felt his heartbeat. It was strong and supportive. He kissed her on the top of the head. "I love you, Faith."

Faith murmured, "I love you too."

"Do you love me enough to trust that I can be strong enough for both of us?"

She pulled away from the hug to look him in the eye.

A twinkle hid behind the steady gaze.

He pressed his finger to his lips and whispered, "Shh."

A sly grin took over his face, and he raised his eyebrows.

The secretive nature sparked Faith's curiosity.

Then he reached into his pocket and pulled out the envelope he showed Faith that first night he saw her. She didn't need to, but she read through the note anyway.

Faith,

When I was thirteen, I knew you would be my wife. I didn't know how or when it would happen. I just knew you would be by my side forever. Our family and friends have been there every step of the way, helping us make the deci-

Paradise Hills Summer

sions that got us to where we are today. For that, I'm thankful. But marriage is between two people. You and me.

I know the flowers, the dress, the food is all for them. As long as you're my wife, I don't care if we have fish, steak, or hot dogs.

Before we get started with them, I want to have an us. A moment when we can say that was the beginning of Clark and Faith Grayson. Meet me at the courthouse on Wednesday at 4:00 for a private ceremony. It'll be just you and me. Then we can have the family and friends show.

I love everything about you.

Clark

He bobbed his chin and wagged his eyebrows. "What do you think?"

His us against the world spirit struck Faith. She was the patient one. He was the one with enduring persistence. Between the two of them, they had the personality to make it through any problem life threw their way. That and they had a shared history to draw upon.

He whispered, "They don't have to know. We can have a barbecue afterward and tell them there."

It was them against the world. Faith wasn't ahead of Clark, nor was he ahead of her. In the corner where she tried to hide from Clark all those weeks ago, they found the missing foundation for their marriage.

She glanced at their mothers chatting about something and

returned to the conversation with Clark. They could pull it off. Faith whispered, "Oh, you sneaky devil."

Clark's raised brows added to the edge of conspiracy. "Are you in?"

She nodded. "Let's do it."

30

AUTHOR'S NOTE

If you know anything about how I write, this is a hiatus, not the end of Clark and Faith's story. They will appear in future books in the Paradise Hills, Montana series. Case in point, Holly and Liam met in the holiday romance novella **Meet Me by The Christmas Tree,** and the wedding occurred six months later in this story. I'll give you a little hint, Clark and Faith will have a Valentine's Day Wedding, and I promise the moms will behave.

I don't know if you caught it, but I named Faith because that was something this main character needed to develop. Because she grew up in Clark's shadow and under her mother's "doting" personality, Faith never had the chance to shine and prove herself to herself. I loved watching her figure it out.

This is where I shamelessly ask you to leave a review of *Paradise Hills Summer*. I read a lot and peruse the reviews before getting that sample chapter. Please let people know if this is a book that would suit their reading style. Tell them it is a clean romance, or that the characters are quirky, or whatever else you look at when choosing a book. Or if you're at a loss for words (I've been there) please, leave some stars.

You made it this far. There is one more link. Mischa and Kellen met in a **short story** exclusive to my reader friends. Now, I have a situation set up to where any person who has read my stories can download it. In other words, you have the choice.

If you choose to join my reader list, you'll get snippets of stories before they launch, notes with stories behind the stories, and short stories long before they make it into an anthology.

Last but not least, please keep in touch. I have a **Facebook page** if you want a peek at the life of someone who lives in rural Montana. Like Faith, I have a **Pinterest account**. That is where I keep track of my characters, recipes, activity ideas...I think you got the idea. In other words, if you want to see the Betsy Grayson potato salad recipe, that's where you'll want to go.

I'LL CLOSE HERE WISHING you love, laughter, and a myriad of smiles. Until *Paradise Hills Trick or Treat*...

Merri

31

WHAT'S NEXT?

PARADISE HILLS TRICK OR TREAT

Who gets mad when someone looks better than their picture?

To bait the right man, Taryn posts older pictures of herself on a dating site. Being a model, she wants someone who will appreciate her for her personality, not her looks. When Taryn matches with Chase, who has been voted Paradise Hills most eligible bachelor three years in a row, she thinks she has found the one.

Chase wants a companion who can also be a friend, and he seems to have found one in Taryn. When she finally agrees to meet him in person after months of relationship building, he is approached by a beautiful woman who looks nothing like the one in her picture. Feeling tricked, he says some things he soon regrets.

With Chase acting nothing like the person she has been chatting with, Taryn is done. He clearly isn't the man she thought he was. But when Chase tries to prove he is the man she fell in love with online, Taryn is in for a treat. Unless the other secrets she kept from him get in the way...

Paradise Hills Trick or Treat is a small town, feel-good, love story that readers of Hallmark Channel stories would enjoy.

CLICK HERE to get your copy of Paradise Hills Trick or Treat so you can continue reading this series today.

32

SNEAK PEEK OF PARADISE HILLS TRICK OR TREAT

This could be the start of something wonderful, or the mistake Taryn would share with her friends over wine. On the other side of the oak wooden doors, her date, Chase Wyngard, was waiting for her. It was in a group setting to eliminate the pressure, but she still had first date jitters.

Taryn Lane stood in front of the Tap House. It was an old railroad station that had been refashioned into a restaurant-style bar that catered to families and beer enthusiast. A group date organized by the Paradise Meet and Greet dating site also presented her with the opportunity to see the often mentioned brewhouse for herself. Taryn meant to check out the place. The group date presented the first opportunity. Anxiousness at what was on the other side of the doors mixed with anticipation had her mind in a jumble.

Her eyes traveled from the polished hardwood floors to red, brick interior walls that matched the exterior of the building. Taryn could tell someone had taken great measures to preserve the building. Distressed wooden tables varied in sizes to accommodate patron's needs. Taryn, knowing what she was looking for, searched out the longest table in the room. Chase told her he'd be sitting on the edge with an empty seat beside him, specifically for her.

Almost immediately, Taryn recognized the sleeve tattoo depicting a mountain landscape. Next, she matched Chase's face with the image on his profile. Despite the cool October weather, Chase wore a short sleeve, V-neck t-shirt. He was cuter in person. That in itself made Taryn feel better. She had shared an older picture of herself and worried about him being upset about the difference from what she shared and what she really looked like. Now that they were meeting in person, they'd have a chance to joke about bad pictures.

To buy herself time, Taryn approached the bar to order her beer first. A line of twenty taps separated her from the brew master. A man who looked to be in his mid-thirties wore a train conductor style cap with Tap House embroidered across the front.

He paused, took a second look at Taryn, and quickly recovered with a smooth grin. "What can I get for you?"

Taryn read through the list on the wall behind him. "I'll have an Octoberfest." She'd sampled the dry, spicy brew when she visited her grandmother's hometown in Germany several years ago. The beer would be a way to possibly connect her past with her future. It had to be a sign that the date would be fun.

"Let me know what you think." The brew master slid the beer over the counter and waited for a response.

"I'm sure I'll like it." Taryn smiled with her eyes. "I've heard good things about what you serve."

He grinned at her compliment, and she turned to meet Chase. Chase didn't notice her until she was beside him. To make sure the space beside him was saved for her, Taryn asked, "Is this seat taken?"

Paradise Hills Summer

With a straight face, Chase replied, "You and I would make beautiful babies."

Taryn almost dropped her beer. She couldn't have heard him correctly.

The man's chiseled jaw and close-shaved, dark blond beard emphasized his condescending smirk.

Yes, he said what she thought he said. Jolts of righteous indignation shot flashes of flaming white light behind her right eye.

For weeks, Chase urged her to join in the group date. In their online chats, he was funny and provocative. He moderated the Meet and Greet site like a father protecting his teenage daughter. Hints at crude comments earned warnings of being banned. His firm responses earned her respect. His no-nonsense approach to topics often launched interesting conversations about dating, friendship, and family life. Occasionally, he posted articles on group date etiquette. With every encounter, Taryn searched for what he was hiding. Nobody could be that perfect and still be single.

In their first conversation, he validated her concerns. Nothing the man in front of her said matched her online crush. Even though he was sitting, he looked tall. His sleeve tattoo added an element of a bad boy that was proud of where he came from. It almost made him irresistible. The glimmer in the back of his eyes taunted her. His comment said it too. She was beneath him.

This was not Taryn's first rodeo. In her modeling days, she dodged the wandering hands of photographers, set designers, even a couple of male models during a photoshoot. They'd whispered, "Just relax and enjoy the party. It'll show the camera we have chemistry." She'd subtly use her knee to create chemistry. It wasn't the chemistry they'd expected, but she made her point.

Taryn never imagined her funny, sweet, mind-your-manners on this forum, Chase would say something so rude. The contradiction log jammed her mind. Taryn pursed her lips and fought through the anger. Something broke loose. She curled the corner of her mouth ever so slightly and leaned closer to Chase. The challenge in his eyes softened to amusement. With it came the answer to her earlier question. The most eligible bachelor of Paradise Hills was single because he was a jerk.

Taryn tipped her mug.

Amusement gave way to disbelief. His jaw dropped when the beer dribbled down the front of his shirt. Taryn tilted the mug further to quicken the flow. It was a slow pour, and she relished every moment. With the last drops of amber liquid landing on his khaki pants, she blew him a kiss.

Chase jumped up out of his chair and threw his arms in the air. "What the hey!" He may have said something a little more colorful, but that was the version Taryn would tell her girlfriends.

She pivoted away from him and sashayed to the counter. The mug released a colorful thud when she set it in front of the brew master. "That was refreshing. Thank you." With a nod, Taryn bid the brew master adieu. She ignored the ruckus behind her and made a beeline to her car.

The cool night air rushed into Taryn as she exited the Paradise Hills Tap House, and the gravity of what she had done hit her. Chase was the moderator of the dating site. She had poured a beer on the lap of the man who had access to all her private information.

Taryn only had one picture on her profile. It was a picture her cousin Gibson took when they were on a hiking trip before her life had been altered by a series of unforeseen circumstances. She hid behind a pair of Oakley sunglasses and a

Paradise Hills Summer

Montana Bobcats baseball cap. Strands of her hair carried by the wind gave her a messy, carefree look. It hid her down to her waist-length wavy, brown hair. Unless Chase looked closely, he wouldn't have noticed her pale biracial skin tone. The sunglasses hid her blue-gray eyes. She posted the innocuous picture to avoid attention like what she had received inside the Tap House.

By the time Taryn reached her car at the edge of the parking lot, the full force of what happened hit her. She had just poured beer on the lap of Paradise Hills most eligible bachelor. Not that he mattered to her. But that might be grounds for a social ostracizing. This time her mind replayed the scene. She couldn't recall if anyone filmed it on their cell phone. The only face that came to her mind was the different variations of Chase.

Disappointment deepened her indignation. Taryn really liked Chase. Not that she saw him with rainbows, unicorns, and wedding bells, but she thought he'd be fun to hang out with. She sat in the driver's seat and sighed. "Oh well, he deserved it."

With the turn of the ignition, the story reached its full circle. She deserved a little of it too. Taryn had broken her own rule. Don't go out alone. Men had been a problem for all her life. For some reason, they thought because she looked in their words, "exotic," they had the right to treat her like she was a creature put on display for their personal delight. They'd caress her arm, touch her hair, or as Chase had done, said things they would never say in front of their mothers or sisters.

Her cousins told her Paradise Hills would be different. "It's a small town where everyone knows everyone," Liam explained. "Once they know you're our family, it will be alright."

"People won't bother you when they know you have four cousins behind you."

"It will be the opposite," Gibson added. "Once they know you're a Lane, you won't be able to get a date. At least that's how it's been for me."

They were wrong. All of them. She ventured out alone because they all had gone on a fly-fishing trip at the Ranch Creek Resort. From now on, she was not going out without one of them as reinforcement. She shifted her car into reverse and left the parking lot.

"WHY ARE PEOPLE CLAPPING?" Chase Wyngard turned red. The small group around him applauded when that crazy, beautiful woman dumped her beer on him. Granted, he deserved it, but they didn't have to be one sided. It was the first thing that popped into his mind, and it came out of his mouth before he had time to take it back. If Chase hadn't known better, he would have sworn a ghost whispered in his ear, and like a child that didn't know better, he'd mimicked what he heard.

The server approached him with a handful of towels, set them on the table, and walked away. Chase took one to wipe off the beer that soaked into his pants and dropped the rest on the floor to soak up the spill. Satisfied that he couldn't be held accountable for a safety hazard, he left the Tap House. Which bummed him for more reasons than he cared to admit. He was there to meet Taryn.

The long-haired siren with lips that begged to be kissed ran interference. He wanted her to get lost before Taryn arrived. If the woman he was waiting for saw him with the woman who looked like she jumped out of a page of a magazine, the date would be over before it started. Taryn would write him off as one of those guys who was distracted by the superficial.

Paradise Hills Summer

He'd been following Taryn on the Paradise Hills Meet and Greet site for weeks. Taryn was active in the forum and took part in the group chats, but she hadn't attended any of the organized events. Chase visited her page so many times his computer prompted him to make it his default home screen. Most of the pictures on her profile were bucket list images. She wanted to go rafting down the Yellowstone River and hike the Rocky Mountains. Only one picture on her page was available to help him find her. It was a picture of her on a hiking trip. Her hair was pulled into a cap, and she wore sunglasses. The way she smiled at whoever was on the other side of the camera had him wanting. He wanted someone to smile at him like that.

In the comfort of his five-bedroom home that needed a wife to help him fill it, Chase ripped off his clothes, showered, and went straight to his computer. As the admin of the Paradise Hills Meet and Greet site, Chase could monitor people's comments. He wanted to see what they said about his early departure from the Tap House. Ten people were logged on to the site, but they were in the middle of a live watch of Aquaman on Netflix. Then he saw the silver lining around the cloud that hovered over his evening. Taryn was in the chat.

She typed #lovethetattoos

Another woman typed: You can have the tattoos. I'll take the rest of him.

A chain of LOLs followed it.

The interaction set Chase's mind at ease. Taryn liked tattoos. He'd have to think of a way to bring it up in a conversation when they finally met. And, if anyone mentioned the beer pour, which they would, he'd have time to post a funny comeback. The night wasn't a total failure. Taryn never showed. So, she hadn't witnessed the encounter with that vixen. He still had a chance to make a good first impression.

THIS IS where the the preview ends. Want more of Taryn and Chase's story. Here is the link to buy Paradise Hills Trick or Treat.

Or you can visit the Small Town Stories Website and read the next chapters.

OTHER BOOKS WRITTEN BY MERRI MAYWETHER

The Paradise Hills, Montana Series

In a cozy town nestled at the foothills of a mountain, love touches the heart of those who seek it.

Meet Me by the Christmas Tree

Paradise Hills Summer

Paradise Hills Trick or Treat

Paradise Hills Thanksgiving

Christmas Wishes

The Ashbrook, Montana Series

While navigating through real-world problems, the friends and family in Ashbrook find second chances at love.

537 Devotion Lane

324 Hope Road

222 Redemption Lane

121 Patience Place

323 Love Lane

452 Memory Lane

202 Canterbury Lane

The Small-Town Stories Series

Light-hearted quick reads for characters within the Ashbrook and Three Creek's, Montana series.

Piece of Cake

Get Well Soon

Just A Friend

For a Visit

The Three Creeks, Montana Series

For a friends to happily ever after romance story, visit Three Creeks, Montana.

Welcome Home

Home Sweet Home

Honey, I'm Home

Home for Good

Hope Springs Series
Sweet Holiday Romance Novellas

Hope Springs Harvest Days

Winter Wonderland Inn

Made in the USA
Middletown, DE
02 October 2023

39953995R00118